"Will you let me make love to you?"

Leon murmured the words huskily.

"No strings attached?" Jemma heard the words leave her lips in the shape of a surrender. "No other lovers?"

"Do you want a deeper commitment from me?"

Jemma thought about it. Thought about the man he was and the power he wielded. "No," she answered. "I want nothing more from you than—this...."

MICHELLE REID grew up on the southern edges of the city of Manchester, England—the youngest in a family of five lively children. But now she lives in the beautiful county of Cheshire, with her executive husband, and they have two grown-up daughters. She loves reading, the ballet and playing tennis when she gets the chance. She hates cooking, cleaning, and despises pressing clothes! Sleep she can do without, and she produces some of her best written work during the early hours of the morning.

Books by Michelle Reid

Don't miss any of our special offers. Write to us at the following address for information on our newest releases.

Harlequin Reader Service
U.S.: 3010 Walden Ave., P.O. Box 1325, Buffalo, NY 14269
Canadian: P.O. Box 609, Fort Erie, Ont. L2A 5X3

MICHELLE REID

Passion Becomes You

Harlequin Books

TORONTO • NEW YORK • LONDON
AMSTERDAM • PARIS • SYDNEY • HAMBURG
STOCKHOLM • ATHENS • TOKYO • MILAN
MADRID • WARSAW • BUDAPEST • AUCKLAND

ISBN 0-373-11752-3

PASSION BECOMES YOU

Copyright © 1994 by Michelle Reid.

First North American Publication 1995.

CHAPTER ONE

JOSH was late in the office on Monday morning—a sure sign that his weekend had been a heavy one.

Jemma's smile was wry as she dealt efficiently with the morning's mail. She had to give it to Cassie Drake— the gorgeous brunette had certainly succeeded where countless before had failed, and managed to keep the equally gorgeous Josh Tanner on a nice rolling boil for three whole months!

A record for him. His women usually lasted only as long as it took him to bed them thoroughly. A low boredom threshold, Josh called it—and the added fact that he couldn't resist trying it on with just about any presentable woman who happened to catch his wandering eye.

Jemma should know—he had tried it on her once or twice. Not that it had worked. She wasn't into men— not men like Josh anyway. He looked at a woman and saw sex with a capital S, and nothing else. He was a rake. A handsome, conceited, feckless rake, and the last type of man she would ever let herself become mixed up with.

She'd already been there—via her father, witnessed what his overactive libido had done to her mother. And no way—no way would she ever let herself fall into that thankless trap.

Josh hadn't given up on her that easily, though, she recalled with a smile. It had taken him two months to accept defeat. Another month to stop sulking about it. And since then—nearly two years ago now—he had made her his best friend and confidante instead.

Which was why she knew all about Cassie, and what she did to him. How just one look at her softly rounded, sensually luxurious figure and his temperature shot off the gauge.

'Why her?' he'd once demanded in sheer exasperated confusion. 'She isn't even my type! I like them tall and slender with legs that go up to their armpits like yours do. And long blonde hair like yours I can strangle myself with!'

'My hair is not blonde, it's sandy.'

'Blonde,' he'd insisted. 'Golden-blonde like honey— hot honey.' His eyes had begun to smoke. 'Makes me want to——'

'Lay one finger on me and I'll tell Cassie!'

It was enough to cool his ardour. 'What is that black-haired witch doing to me?' he'd muttered and slammed away to his own office to brood.

Jemma thought she had the answer to that question, but refused to offer it to him. It would be bad enough working with him once he discovered it for himself without her bringing forward the dreadful day. But, in her opinion, Josh Tanner, the sexy blond rake of London town, had met his Waterloo—and at the hands of a woman who made no secret of what she wanted from Josh.

'Marriage, children—the full works,' she'd told Jemma recently while sitting on the corner of her desk waiting for Josh to take her to lunch. 'I'm sick of playing the field. And anyway, I'm getting on.' It seemed that in this day and age twenty-seven was really getting on by the expression on Cassie's face when she said it. 'So I started looking around me for a suitable candidate.'

Which happened to be Josh, something Jemma found rather strange since she considered her boss the last man on earth a woman would actually want to settle down with. After all, a rake was a rake in her book. Good fun to be with, great in bed, so the tale went, but not—definitely not—husband material.

'I happened to meet Josh at a party I'd gone to with an old friend of mine,' she'd gone on. 'Fell for the self-obsessed jerk on the spot and would have had to be blind not to understand the lecherous look in Josh's eyes. The air fairly sizzled between us, highly amusing Leon, I can tell you—you know Leon Stephanades?' she'd asked, and at Jemma's blank look had added, 'Darling, you do not know what you're missing. If I'd dared to set my sights so high, I would have gone all out to catch him instead of Josh. But Leon is—special. Very Greek. Very wealthy. And very, very possessive of his freedom. His father has tried all ways—threats, bribes, you name it—to get his son to marry the nice Greek girl with the hefty dowry he has picked out for him, but Leon refuses to so much as consider it. Caused quite a family rift, so I gather.' Her beautifully sculptured brows had arched ruefully, the reason why coming in the next sentence. 'So what chance does a not-so-nice English girl with nothing to offer him but a great body have against all of that? None,' she'd answered her own question. 'So I decided to go all out to catch Josh instead. Leon and I are still good friends, though—which Josh hates,' she'd added with a grin that was all feminine guile. 'He's as jealous as sin of Leon because he thinks we had something going between us once, which is not true,' she had insisted, though her expression had implied that she maybe would have liked it to be true. 'But his jealousy is probably the only ray of hope he allows me in this crazy relationship we're having—that and the fact he can't get enough of me,' she'd tagged on ruefully. 'Leon says if I land Josh Tanner he'll buy us a twelve-inch solid gold flying pig for a wedding present, because that's how much of a chance he thinks I've got of pulling it off! But I'm working on it,' she had concluded determinedly.

Cassie must have told Josh more or less the same thing, because it was only a few days after that conversation with Cassie that Josh had come striding into the office, growling, 'I'm not marrying any woman! Not even for a solid gold pig!'

The phone began to ring now. Jemma picked up the receiver to have the familiar impatient bark of Josh Tanner hit her eardrums. 'I'm late,' he stated the obvious. 'I've had one hell of a weekend. Only just woken up. You're going to have to hold the fort until I can get there.'

'What about your ten o'clock appointment with that big cheese from the Leonadis Corporation?' she reminded him, glancing at her watch only to confirm that it was already twenty to ten. There was no way Josh could make it here in time.

Some very unsavoury vocabulary came slashing down the line. He had obviously forgotten all about the appointment. Not like Josh, she acknowledged. It had to have been a hell of a weekend. 'Him of all people,' he muttered. 'That's all I need today. Look, you're going to have to try and put him off,' he added impatiently. 'See if you can catch him before he leaves his office. Make my excuses. And if that conniving bitch I've been seeing turns up—tell her I've died and gone to hell! And not to bother following me!'

'Who?' she asked, frowning. 'Cassie?'

But Jemma was already talking to fresh air. Josh had slammed down the phone. She sat staring at the contraption for the space of ten seconds while trying to make head or tail of that final scathing remark, then shrugged, replacing her own receiver. It seemed that when Josh had said he'd had a hell of a weekend he'd meant it.

The lovers' bed must have had thorns in it, she mused, and smiled to herself as she hunted out the number of the Leonadis Corporation.

It was only as she waited for someone to answer that she realised she had no idea what the managing director's name was. Josh had made the appointment himself on Friday. And all he had said was, 'I hate the damned man, but he's hunting for new outlets to get his design components from and I need the business. So I suppose I'll have to fanny round him.'

She grimaced, wondering what the man could have done to Josh to make him dislike him so much; her boss was not normally drawn to taking personal exception to potential clients. In fact, he was usually quite happy to 'fanny round' anyone so long as it brought him business.

'The Leonadis Corporation?'

Jemma blinked. 'Ah,' she began, wondering how to get around this one without sounding like a fool. She explained who she was and why she was ringing, then added, 'So I hoped to catch your managing director before he leaves the building,' she concluded, mentally crossing her fingers that the receptionist on the other end would provide the name and save her having to ask.

'Oh, I'm afraid you may be too late,' she was informed. 'But I'll put you through to his secretary.'

'Thank you.' Jemma held the line while she waited to be transferred, but a single glance at her watch told her she was running out of time. 'Damn you, Josh,' she muttered to herself.

'Mr Stephanades's secretary speaking. Can I help you?'

Stephanades—now where had she heard that name before? 'I do hope so,' she said, then quickly went into her explanation again. 'Mr Stephanades had an appointment with Mr Tanner for ten o'clock this morning, but I am afraid Mr Tanner has been delayed. Am I too late to save him a wasted journey?'

'When I am already standing right here, I would say yes, you are much too late,' a deep, smooth, beautifully

accented and drily amused voice drawled at her from
across the room.

Startled, Jemma glanced up—then felt everything vital
inside her grind to a shuddering halt when she found
herself staring at the most disturbingly attractive man
she had ever seen in her life!

He was leaning in the open doorway, hands shoved
into the pockets of his dark silk business suit trousers
so that the side panels of his jacket had been shoved out
of the way to expose the solid breadth of his chest beneath the crisp clean whiteness of his shirt. He was tall
and dark, his black hair cut in a short, neat style which
kept the hint of a wave contained to the silken top of
his head. His bone-structure was square and strong, the
skin stretched across it smooth and tanned. Black eyes
were teasing her from between jet-black, sleepily curling
lashes. And he was smiling at her with the most star-
tlingly sensual mouth she had ever encountered.

Faultless, she decided hazily. He is absolutely faultless.
He set her blood pumping in a way which left her in no
doubt whatsoever as to what was happening to her. And
the dark, coiling warmth she was experiencing in the pit
of her stomach confirmed it.

This, she accepted, as she continued to stare breathlessly at him, was what it was all about.

Attraction. Dark and hot and rousing.

Her continued silence sent his sleek brows arching.
Jemma heaved in a deep breath of air in an effort to
pull herself together. The action lifted her breasts in a
slow quivering motion beneath her white silky blouse
then dropped them again in the same tremulous way,
making those gorgeous lashes of his fall in two luxurious
curves over his eyes as he followed the revealing motion.
Her nipples stung painfully in response, and she blushed
hotly with embarrassment, wishing for the first time ever
that she possessed such a thing as a bra, because she

didn't have to look down at herself to know what he was witnessing happening to her.

'Miss Davis?' a slightly puzzled voice prompted in her ear.

'I...' She ran the tip of her tongue around her suddenly parched lips. 'It—it doesn't matter,' she whispered breathlessly and replaced the receiver without really knowing she had done it, her eyes not leaving the man leaning in the doorway.

The smile widened on his lips, giving them a sensually knowing quality that annoyed her even as she accepted his right to display it. She knew who he was, of course. He had made that clear when he let her know he was there. But she could not for the life of her respond with anything like the light brisk, 'Good morning, Mr Stephanades!' Josh would expect of her. She wanted to know his first name, to feel it curl off her tongue like a caress. Her heart was bursting, her breasts tingling, her calves and thighs trembling with the full fermenting blast of his attraction.

'Shall we leave now, or do you need a few moments longer to compose yourself?'

'W-what?' She blinked, blue eyes filling with bewildered confusion. 'L-leave for where?'

'My apartment,' he explained, levering himself away from the door-frame to come further into the room, closing the door behind him. 'I must say,' he went on lightly before Jemma had a chance to digest the full import of his first remark, 'I have in my life been propositioned in many ways, but never with such open and—dare I say it?—helpless invitation before. I find it rather—enchanting.'

Stung, Jemma closed her eyes, feeling the heat of embarrassed colour grow hotter in her cheeks.

'I'm so sorry,' she murmured, pulling herself together with an effort that cost her her dignity as she stumbled shakily to her feet. 'You took me by surprise, Mr...'

She'd forgotten his name. His secretary had only just informed her of it, and already in her stupidity she had forgotten it!

'Stephanades,' he supplied it for her, the mockery spiked and cruel. 'Leon Stephanades, at your service, Miss...?'

Leon, his first name was Leon. Jemma actually had to count to ten to stop herself repeating the name in the breathless little way she knew was hanging on the very end of her dry, quivering tongue.

On a jerky movement she straightened her body, 'Davis,' she supplied, lifting her chin to face him as coolly as she could, but she knew the hectic flush still colouring her cheeks said it all. 'I'm sorry you've had a wasted journey, sir.' That's better, Jemma, she told herself encouragingly, refusing to look anywhere but at the left tip of his well shaped ear in case the look in his eyes sent her crazy again. 'But Mr Tanner has been delayed and cannot make your appointment. I was hoping to catch you before you left your office, but as we both see——' she tried a wry smile and it just about worked '—I was too late.'

'How fortunate.'

Oh, good grief! She almost choked in appalled horror when his reply made her breasts tingle again. She closed her eyes, only opening them again when she was sure she was looking down at her desk and not at him. 'If you will just give me a moment,' she murmured a trifle hoarsely, feeling a fool—a damned fool, 'I'll find Mr Tanner's appointment book and we can arrange another——'

'I have a better idea,' he cut in. 'Meet me for lunch and we will discuss... arrangements over a light meal and a bottle of wine.'

Jemma almost died inside with shame, not in any way missing the double meaning. 'I'm sorry.' She stuck to the official meaning in his words with all the secretarial cool she could muster, but it wasn't easy when her body was responding wildly to the other. 'S-someone has to m-man the office when Mr Tanner isn't here.'

'Shame,' he murmured, so softly that her eyes flickered up to clash with his, and her cheeks went even hotter at the expression on his face. This was not all one-sided. He was attracted to her also. 'For I am flying to New York this afternoon and will not be back for at least a week. A long time to leave something like this— pending...'

Suddenly, the office door flew open again, and Jemma looked towards it in wild hope that it was Josh come to rescue her.

But it wasn't Josh. It was Cassie, looking as mad as hell. 'Where is that low-down, no-good son of a——?' She stopped mid-flow, her unusually pale face lighting up when she saw the man standing in the centre of Jemma's office. 'Leon!' she cried, and threw herself into his arms.

It was at that moment, and only that moment, that Jemma's addled brain made the connection it should have made long, humiliating minutes ago. Leon. Cassie's good friend, Leon.

And their mutual affection showed in the way he gathered Cassie into his arms then kissed her warmly on both cheeks before smiling indulgently down at her.

Jealousy whipped through Jemma like a flash fire, contracting her nerve-ends until she could barely breathe across the acid taste of it filling her mouth. If Josh had ever seen them together like this, it was no wonder he was so jealous.

At least Josh has the right to be jealous, a little voice taunted inside her burning head. You don't.

You don't even know the man!

God in heaven! She sat down heavily in her chair, trying desperately to throw off what was happening to her. She wanted to scratch Cassie's eyes out. She wanted to drag her away from him. Scratch his eyes out!

'How's your love-life?' he was saying teasingly to Cassie.

She pulled a wry face and wound her arms more tightly around his neck. 'Not so good that this isn't welcome,' she said very drily. 'More than welcome...'

'Tanner not treating you well?' The mocking brow lifted questioningly.

Cassie's beautiful mouth took a downward turn. 'He's a rat of the first order,' she scowled, her dark eyes flashing bitterly. 'And I hate him!'

Jemma started at the other woman's virulence. Leon Stephanades frowned. 'Trouble?' he asked.

'Big trouble,' Cassie said ominously, and pulled out of his arms to turn on Jemma. 'Where is he?' she demanded. 'Skulking in some dark hole somewhere, waiting for the bogy-man to go away?'

Jemma opened her mouth to answer, wondering curiously just what had happened this weekend to make both Josh and Cassie this mad.

'He's...' She was about to trot out the same excuse for Josh she had given to Leon Stephanades when the phone began to ring. Absently she picked up the receiver and chanted out the usual.

'Did you catch him before he left?' Josh's impatient bark made her jump, and she pressed the earpiece tighter to her ear in an attempt to block Josh's voice off.

'Er—no,' she answered carefully. 'Can—can I call you back?'

Josh had never been slow on the uptake, and he wasn't now. 'He's already there?'

'Yes.'

'Damn...' There was a pause, then Josh muttered something and grunted. 'You'd better put him on so I can apologise personally.'

'I—er don't think that would be a very good idea at the moment,' she said, lowering her eyes and her voice from the two watchful people listening to her to add, 'We're not alone.'

She didn't hear Josh's answer to that, because Cassie had leapt at her desk, eyes flashing green fire—and something else that Jemma could not interpret but hinted oddly at terror. 'Is that Josh? Give me that!' she demanded, trying to snatch the phone from Jemma. 'I have a few things I want to——'

'I don't want to speak to her!' Josh grated into Jemma's ear.

'Give, Jemma!' Cassie insisted, her eyes fire-bright with anger. 'It's time that rat learned a few home truths!'

'Get her out of my office—now!' Josh barked.

'I can't!' she answered both of them, jumping to her feet in an effort to stop Cassie from wrenching the phone from her, and Josh hurled out a string of abuse aimed entirely at Cassie while Leon Stephanades viewed the whole scene with a look of lazy amusement sparking his eyes.

Jemma hated him at that moment. The whole thing was utterly ridiculous. She felt stupid being a part of it, and he thought it was funny!

He glanced up at her then, caught the look burning in her eyes, and suddenly the amusement left him to allow something so elemental to take its place that she gasped as everything inside her went haywire in answer to it, heart, lungs, pulses, even her skin—as if every minute hair follicle she possessed had been delivered an electric shock which set her whole body tingling.

Josh was growling, Cassie was shouting, but suddenly they might as well not have been there for all Jemma knew. She was lost in a seething hot raid on her senses, and what really threw her into hectic confusion was the fact that he was feeling the exact same way—and doing nothing whatsoever to hide it!

Then it all came crashing in. With the help of a sudden pained cry from Cassie, Jemma refocused her attention on the other woman just in time to hear her choke, 'Whatever I am, you bastard, I am still pregnant with your child!' Then she crumpled on to the floor.

In a state of stunned shock, Jemma watched the lightning-quick reactions of Leon Stephanades as he caught Cassie's weight before she hit the floor, listened to Josh cursing and swearing on the other end of the line, his voice so thick that it was obvious he was feeling the pressure of his emotions as much as Cassie was.

'The bitch trapped me, Jemma,' he was saying hoarsely. 'She deliberately laid a trap for me.'

Jemma did not know what to say. In the end, she just murmured, 'I'll call you back, Josh. I'll call you back,' and slowly replaced the receiver.

By the time she had collected a cool cloth and a glass of water, Cassie was beginning to show signs of life. Leon Stephanades had carried her into Josh's office and placed her on the leather sofa in there and was now squatting beside her, gently chafing at one of her hands.

Jemma knelt down beside him and offered him the cloth. He took it without speaking, his expression grim to say the least as he applied the cloth to Cassie's brow.

It was him Cassie saw when she eventually opened her eyes. 'Oh, God, Leon,' she whispered tragically. 'What am I going to do?'

'Nothing, until you feel well enough,' he answered calmingly. 'Then I will take you home.'

Tears blurred the wretched green of her eyes. 'I didn't do it on purpose,' she claimed fretfully.

'Didn't you?' he said. That was all, but even as Jemma stiffened in violent protest at what his tone was implying Cassie's eyes were going dark with guilt, and on a pained choke she hid her face in her hands and began to sob wretchedly.

Shocked, Jemma sat back on her heels, the fact that any woman would set out deliberately to trap a man that way just too awful for her to take in.

Leon Stephanades turned his head to look at her, then grimaced. 'Don't look so appalled, Miss Davis,' he drawled. 'Your sex use this ploy all the time. To them, it is the next best thing to a genuine proposal—especially when it is a man like your Mr Tanner who is involved. Or me,' he then tagged on cynically.

Feeling sick, Jemma got up and walked back into her own office. She felt ashamed of her sex, if what Leon Stephanades had said was true. Ashamed for Cassie whom she had liked and even admired for what she'd seen as her candid honesty about her intentions.

And Josh? She sat down behind her desk and wondered what she felt for Josh.

She felt sorry for him, she realised. For the first time in two years of witnessing the way he used women for his own purposes, she actually felt sorry for him.

Because, no matter how much he deserved his comeuppance in one way or another, he did not deserve this.

The phone rang. And for the next few minutes she had to turn her attention strictly to business as a spate of calls followed one on top of the other.

She was just replacing the receiver for the final time when Leon Stephanades came through to her office. 'She is calmer now,' he said. 'When she has tidied herself, I will take her home.'

Jemma nodded dumbly, refusing to look at him, shock and distaste at what Cassie had done still evident on her face. He studied her for a moment, then closed the connecting door between the two offices and walked over to her desk.

'Are you all right?' he asked.

'I just find it hard to believe she actually did it deliberately,' she confessed.

'Women are devious creatures, Miss Davis,' he said heavily. 'They will go to any lengths to achieve their own ends.'

'Thank you.' She smiled tightly. 'Generalisations like that keep the world turning, I suppose.'

'They do in my sphere,' he said cynically.

His sphere—who the hell did he think he was? Were all women supposed to be as unscrupulous as Cassie? 'Well,' she said, coming stiffly to her feet and making a play of gathering her telephone notes together, 'I shall try to remember that when I decide to go hunting, and make a wide berth of your—sphere.'

'Now that,' he murmured, 'would be a great pity.'

She glanced up, drawn by the husky message in his voice. Their eyes clashed, and she stopped breathing, drowning instead in the dark, deep promise burning in his eyes.

No, she told herself from some hazy distance in the back of her foggy mind. Don't let this happen. Think of Cassie weeping in the next room. Think of Josh, just another version from the same mould as this man. Ruthless, selfish women-eaters.

He reached across the desk and touched a thumb to her mouth, drawing it downwards to part her lips a little. The softly padded flesh beneath his touch grew hot as blood began pumping into it, swelling it, assailing her with the most erotically sensual experience of her life.

'No strings,' he murmured so softly that she barely caught the words above the sudden roaring inside her head. 'No commitments other than that while we are together we neither of us turn to anyone else. When it is over, we part honestly, as friends. I will be your only lover. And I will give myself exclusively to you.'

The hand moved, sliding beneath her hair to curve her nape, then he was leaning towards her, drawing her towards him across the width of the desk, and he replaced the caressing finger with his mouth. It was cool and firm, her own hot and excruciatingly sensitised flesh contracting in reaction so that she jumped, startled as if stung.

'Think about it,' he murmured as he drew away again. 'And I will call you soon. Now.' While she blinked, still lost in the sensual daze he had so easily wrapped around her, Leon Stephanades straightened up and became the cool businessman. 'I will take Cassandra home. Tell Tanner I will be out of the country for a about a week. If he wishes to deal with me then he had better be available when I get back.' He turned to go back to Josh's office, then spun back again, his expression darkening when he saw how thoroughly he had incapacitated her, but that was all; he gave no other indication that he had just made the most audacious proposition Jemma had ever heard. 'You can also tell him that, no matter what his decision will be about Cassandra's condition, as her good friend, I expect her to be treated with respect. She is only human, after all, and humans are by nature fallible.'

CHAPTER TWO

'FALLIBLE?' Josh snarled, prowling around his office like an angry bull. 'The bitch isn't fallible. She's like an armoured tank, equipped with the most modern killing devices known to man!'

He had been in the office ten minutes—arriving just ten minutes after Leon had taken a wilting Cassie away.

'She said to tell you she'd be in touch.' Jemma relayed that message too. But she did not inject the same amount of tight defiance into it that Cassie had done. She hadn't dared. As it was, he hit the roof.

'I don't wish to set eyes on the conniving bitch again!' he bit out, then swung on Jemma, his grey eyes as hard and as sharp as glass. 'Did she tell you she did it deliberately?'

Jemma nodded. 'Leon Stephanades got it out of her.'

'And how fortunate for her that he was around!' The jeer was bitter and cutting. 'For all I know, they probably planned it between them!'

'What, that man aiding and abetting in stitching up another of his kind?' She only heard her own contempt once the words had left her tongue. 'He would rather cut his own throat first!'

'And what do you know about him?' Josh challenged deridingly. 'As far as I am aware, you only met him for the first time today.'

And what a meeting, Jemma thought with a small shiver. 'It doesn't take much to recognise the type, Josh,' she murmured drily. 'I recognised it in you on first sighting, too.'

His eyes sharpened, something in her tone diverting his attention from his own problems for a moment. 'Proposition you, did he?' he mocked. She blushed— enough of an answer in itself. 'Well, I hope you had the good sense to give him the same put-down you gave me,' he said grimly. 'Because that guy is big-league. He plays to different rules from the rest of us.'

'As far as I can see,' she retaliated, simply because she felt uncomfortable in knowing that, far from putting Leon Stephanades down, she had virtually thrown herself at him, 'you're both tarred with the same brush!'

'Only he's a darn sight more powerful than me,' Josh pointed out.

'How powerful?' Jemma asked curiously, beginning to tingle again, just talking about him.

'Among the top twenty richest families in the world— that powerful,' Josh answered, then ran his fingers through his straight blond hair in frustration. 'And God help any woman who tried to pull Cassie's dirty trick on him!' he grunted, slumping down in a chair.

'Josh...' Jemma put out a hand to touch his arm in appeal. 'Cassie loves you! I know she does! What she's done is stupid and wrong,' she acknowledged. 'But I am sure she did it out of love! Doesn't that count for anything?'

He shook his head. 'Does love deceive, Jemma?' he challenged. 'Does it betray trust, connive to trap? Is it selfish and greedy and bloody ruthless?'

'I don't know,' she replied, hurting for him because she could see the real hurt his anger was trying to hide. 'Because I've never been in love to know.'

'I feel betrayed,' he confessed. 'Bloody betrayed!'

They sat in dull silence for a while after that, Jemma completely sympathising with Josh even though she could partly understand Cassie's motives. The woman had not tried to hide her ultimate goal, after all. Marriage and children. The full works. But the really sad fact

among all of it was that Jemma had a sneaking suspicion that Cassie would have got it all from Josh if
she'd only been a bit more patient. He'd been crum-
bling, she was sure of it. But now...?

'What are you going to do?' she asked him huskily.

He sighed and got up. 'I don't know,' he answered
flatly. 'All I do know is that she's had it as far as I—
me personally—am concerned. She's pregnant; there isn't
a damned thing I can do about that now. If she wants
to keep it, then I'll support her and it. If she wants an
abortion, then I'll pay for it. But if she wants me, she
can go to hell before she'll get me again.'

Fagged to death by the time she let herself into her
flat that night, Jemma just dropped her bag and sank
into the nearest chair. They had managed to get some
work done during the afternoon, but not much, and what
there was had been achieved in a grim mutual silence
that had eventually left its mark on her throbbing head.

Trina walked into the room, chewing on a banana.
'Bad day?' she enquired when she saw Jemma's drained
face.

'Hmm,' was all she could manage.

'Want cheering up?' Trina, the sexiest Mrs Mop in the
domestic cleaning game, tended to finish work several
hours before Jemma, simply because most people liked
their homes cleaned and vacated before three o'clock in
the afternoon. She ran her own business from the flat
with the help of a veritable army of part-timers who
worked in teams, and not one of them wore a turban on
her head or dared have a cigarette hanging out of the
corner of her mouth. They wore uniforms which rivalled
the smartest airline ones, and they travelled around in
neat little vans with neat little smiles and a brisk friendly
manner. They were all paid well, but then Trina's charges
were high. You get what you pay for, was her motto,
and London, especially up-market London, had accepted and acknowledged that long ago. Trina had a

waiting-list of potential clients almost as long as her list of real ones. She'd wanted to expand at one time, but the current recession had put paid to that idea—that and her super-sharp accountant-cum-boyfriend Frew. Trina was a tall, slim, easygoing redhead, with green eyes, a sharp tongue and a nasty sense of humour.

Jemma opened her eyes long enough to scrutinise Trina's deadpan face, then closed them again and shook her head. 'Not tonight, thank you,' she refused the offer. 'I don't think I'm up to one of your nice surprises.'

'Shame,' Trina pouted. 'Because this one is rather a cut above the ordinary. Still...' Jemma sensed her friend's shrug as she turned to leave the sitting-room-cum-office again '...I suppose it will keep.'

Jemma sighed, remained exactly where she was and how she was for the space of thirty delicious seconds, then sighed again and hauled herself out of the chair. 'All right!' she called after Trina. 'You win! I can't stand not knowing. What's the nice——? My God!' she choked. 'Where did those come from?'

She had walked out of the sitting-room and down the hall to the kitchen while she was talking; now she just stood, rooted to the spot in the kitchen doorway, staring at the largest basket of out-of-season fruit and flowers she had ever seen.

'Looking at them,' Trina said sardonically, 'from all over the world, I'd say.'

It filled their small kitchen table. The basket, an exquisitely woven affair of rich golden cane with a tall rounded handle, simply spilled over with flowers. Pretty, star-shaped lilies, sensually scented pure white jasmine, blood-red hibiscus heads that were almost too heavy for their stems. Pink, purple and the palest lilac sprays of bougainvillaea clustered everywhere, and at the base were oranges with the dark green leaves still attached to their short stems. Peaches as big as grapefruits. Grapes, green and black, in huge, succulent bunches. And figs, fresh, plump, juicy figs that made the mouth water just to look at them.

There was a card. Trina plucked it from the centre and mockingly passed it over to Jemma. 'For you, ma'am,' she drawled, watching her face as she took the card then dragged her rounded eyes down to focus on it. 'Methinks you have a passionate admirer. The writing on the envelope is sexy, too,' she pointed out. 'All sharp strokes and dramatic curves. I wonder who it can be?'

Jemma wasn't listening. She was trembling instead, staring at the envelope and frightened to open it. She knew who it was from; there was a little voice inside her head repeating his name over and over again. How he had found out her address she had no idea, but that cynical part in her she hadn't known existed until today was telling her that for a man like him it wouldn't be that hard.

What had Josh said about him? From one of the richest families in the world, was what he had said. Powerful. A man not to mess around with.

And Cassie? What had she said about him? Sexy. Loyal. Invincible. Even his own father could not dictate to him.

And what have you learned about him yourself, Jemma? she asked herself shakily. Beautiful, she replied. Dangerous. Fair-minded but cocksure and arrogant with it. Determined, if this basket was a sign of determination to get his own way. Honest, if his proposition was serious. Deadly, if her own tangled feelings were anything to go by. He had succeeded in tying her in sensual knots within seconds of setting eyes on him.

She sucked in a shaky breath, her fingers trembling as she slowly broke the seal on the envelope and took out the gold-embossed card inside.

The words blurred then slowly cleared before her wary eyes.

Today was no way to meet someone who is destined to become the most important person in my life. It was a day of bad smells and acid tastes. So I send you these. Fruits to sweeten your mouth and the flowers of my homeland to freshen the air around you. Keep the flowers warm and moist or they will wither and die before I can see you again. Eat the fruit, enjoy the sensual tastes of my native land and think of me. Leon.

The air left her lungs on a tremulous sigh as she looked back at the basket filling the table, only to find its beauty superimposed by his darkly attractive and smoulderingly sensual face.

God in heaven. She pulled out a chair and sat down, the hand holding the card going up to cover her eyes.

'Bad news, then—not good?' Trina prompted, curious at Jemma's reaction.

She held out the card for her friend to take. 'Beware of Greeks bearing gifts,' she murmured, and left Trina to make of that what she may.

'Who is this Leon?' she asked after smothering several muffled chokes as she read the blatantly evocative words. 'I've never heard you mention a Leon before.'

'That's because I hadn't met him before today,' Jemma explained, and sat back in the chair, grateful to find his face had disappeared from the basket. 'He is one Leon Stephanades. A—business colleague of Josh's.'

'Wow,' Trina gasped, and sank down in the other chair.

'You've already heard of him, I see,' Jemma mocked.

Trina nodded. 'But Jemma,' she exclaimed, searching her friend's face worriedly, 'he's way out of our league, love!'

'I know it.' A funny expression crossed Jemma's face; she didn't even recognise it herself, except that it felt as if it came somewhere close to desolation. 'But try telling my senses that, will you?' She grimaced self-deridingly. 'I made an utter fool of myself today, Tri,' she confessed. 'He walked into Josh's office and I felt the earth move beneath me! I couldn't stop staring at him!' Her expression was pained. 'I couldn't think! I couldn't breathe! I couldn't even focus! There were birds flying around in my head and puffy white clouds floating across my vision! He smiled and my heart did somersaults! And—God,' she choked, covering her face with her hands, 'he would have had to be blind not to know what was happening to me!'

'Well,' Trina murmured slowly, looking down at the card still in her hand, 'he must have experienced something similar to respond with this.'

'Did he?' Her expression was cynical to say the least. 'What he saw, Tri, was a peach ripe for the plucking!' She picked a peach from the basket and brandished it bitterly in front of her. 'And does a man like that turn an easy meal down? Does he hell!' she answered herself scathingly. 'And he's all man, Tri,' she added helplessly. 'Big, tough and lean. So damned attractive he knocks your eyes out, and so disgustingly sure of himself that he quite coolly propositioned me!' The contempt was back, but aimed at Leon instead of herself this time.

'How?' Trina's eyes were round like saucers and eager with interest.

'How does a man like that proposition a potential lover?' Jemma snapped. 'He laid down the ground rules. If you want to play in my league then this is how it's done—and so on. I wanted to slap his arrogant face, but all I did do was let him kiss me!' Self-disgust rattled in her throat. 'By the time he let me up for air again, I was so dizzy I couldn't think, never mind hit out!'

'So?' Trina prompted. 'How did it get to the point that he sends you something like this?' she wanted to know. 'And I don't mean the basket—I mean this card. It reads like a *fait accompli* to me—except the talk about smells and acid, of course,' she frowned, not able to work that bit out. 'He expects to see you, Jemma, when he gets back from wherever he's gone off to. A man doesn't make that assumption unless you've let him.'

'This one does,' she grunted. 'Especially when the girl in question gave him no encouragement to think otherwise.'

'You mean—you just let him get away with kissing you and propositioning you like that?'

'I would have let him take me on the office floor if he'd wanted to,' Jemma said drily. 'That was the level I'd sunk to!'

'My God!' Trina sat back and stared. 'I can't believe it! Wait till I tell Frew! He'll go bananas! He claims the man hasn't been born who can get through your thick shell!'

'Well, thanks very much, Frew!' Jemma cried. 'And what gives him the right to think he knows anything at all about me?'

'Come off it, Jemma!' Trina scoffed. 'You and me both know you're as picky as a worm in a barrel of apples! How many twenty-four-year-old virgins do you think Frew knows?'

'That's a horrible thing to say!' Jemma flared, jumping to her feet and dropping the lovely peach on to the table. The soft velvet skin split open, allowing the sweet, sensual scent of its juicy fruit to seep out. It assailed her nostrils, whetted her tastebuds, and she had to close her eyes because she was suddenly thrown into a storm of sensation that was all directed by one cleverly manipulative man.

'Your parents are entirely to blame for that!' Trina went on, unaware of the torment going on inside Jemma. 'If it wasn't your father having some torrid affair with another woman it was your mother paying him back by putting it about with some other man! What an example they set you! And now look at you!' she exclaimed.

'You're standing there, trembling with indignation over Frew's impression of you when you know damned well it's only the truth! You're afraid of starting your sexual ball rolling, Jemma,' she stated bluntly, 'just in case you discover that you've got more of your parents in you than you can deal with!'

'Do you want me to bed the very next man who walks in that door just to prove you wrong?' she flared, her eyes snapping open to glare at her so-called best friend.

Trina's mouth twitched. 'Not if it's my Frew, you'd better not,' she warned. 'Or it will be your first and last experience.'

'Oh, go to hell, Tri,' Jemma sighed, deflated by her flatmate's unfailing sense of humour.

'Don't you see what's happened to you today, Jemma?' Trina appealed on a more serious note. 'You've been so determined to keep your emotions under a tight lid that when a man like Leon Stephanades came along your senses boiled up and the lid flew off so they all came shooting out like steam under pressure! That's why you made such a damned fool of yourself with him!'

'Thanks for the analysis,' Jemma grunted, and sat down again. 'You've made me feel so much better!'

'I was not attempting to make you feel better,' Trina sighed. 'Only understand why you responded to him as you did! The man is a god among men. You've ambled along quite nicely while only confronted with mere mortals, but when it came to a godlike being you blew your emotional top!'

'Josh would not take kindly to being classed as mere mortal,' Jemma pointed out.

'Josh Tanner,' Trina stated deridingly, 'does not even get a look-in compared to your Leon.'

'Tell that to Cassie,' Jemma grimaced. And she told Trina the rest of what had happened today.

'Oh, my,' her friend drawled when she finished. 'Now I see what your Leon means when he writes about nasty tastes and smells. The whole thing stinks and tastes bad.'

'He is not *my* Leon!' Jemma angrily pointed out.

'No?' Trina quizzed. 'Then what are you going to do about him?'

'Nothing,' she shrugged. 'Just ignore him until he goes away.'

But that was not as easy as it sounded. Mainly because Leon Stephanades refused to be ignored. Over the coming week, Jemma was barraged with reminders of his existence and his intentions.

First there was a long velvet case hand-delivered to her flat with the logo of a very exclusive jeweller embossed on its lid. It contained a fine gold bracelet, linked at its clasp by a single turquoise. 'The colour of your eyes, don't you agree?' the accompanying note said. Jemma closed the lid and put it away, determined to give it back to him at the first opportunity she got. The next day came the matching earrings. On Thursday the matching necklace. 'Wear them for me on our first night together,' the accompanying note said.

Her mouth tightened, the idea that he thought he could buy her like this filling her with an icy anger, and she discarded the necklace into her dressing-table drawer with the same contempt with which she had discarded the bracelet and earrings. On Friday there was nothing. No special delivery to come home to, no note, nothing. Trina studied her face sagely, and Jemma lifted her chin in a defiant refusal to utter a single word.

That night she accepted a date with a man who had just moved into the flat below. He was an architect, just finding his feet in the big London company he had recently joined. He was good-looking, pleasant and companionable, and by the time the evening was drawing to a close Jemma was beginning to feel at peace with herself for the first time in a week.

If it hadn't been bad enough having Leon obsess her every waking thought, then trying to work with Josh in the mood he was in had been just as bad. Not that she blamed him for it—he had every right to behave like a bear with a sore head. But Cassie's constant phone calls, pleading to speak with him, had taken their toll on Jemma's nerves. And when his persistent refusal to speak to her had only had Cassie pouring out her heart on Jemma's ears instead, the tension inside her had begun to hit an all-time high.

So she was quite happy to give herself up to the light, congenial company of Tom MacDonald. As his name suggested, he was a Scot, and eager to make new friends. They talked about anything and everything over a quiet dinner in a small Italian restaurant a short walk away from their flats. He told her about his life in a small Scottish village just outside Edinburgh where his rector father and forbearing mother had reared a family of six boisterous children in the big, rambling vicarage home, and where he had sometimes been willing to sell his soul for a bit of privacy. And she told him about her life as an only child who'd spent her childhood worrying which of her parents was going to walk out next—or, worse, whether they both would at the same time. It surprised her that she told him all of this since the only other person she had ever discussed her lonely uncertain childhood with had been Trina—or maybe, she decided later, it was because of what Trina had said to her the other night that had made her open up to Tom. Whatever. By the time they walked back home, she was feeling comfortable enough to make another date with him for the next night.

They parted at his flat door since it was on a lower landing than her own, and she let him kiss her, half relieved, half disappointed that fireworks had not gone off in her head as they had done when Leon had kissed her.

Trina was still up when she got in, reclining across Frew, who was stretched out on the sofa watching the end of a cops and robbers film.

'Guess who's been calling you all night?' Trina taunted lazily.

Jemma went cold inside. 'I've no idea,' she said, hoping to God that she was right, and she didn't know.

'Mr Macho Stephanades himself, no less.' Frew dashed Jemma's hopes in one sardonically uttered sentence. 'I answered the last time,' he told her drily. 'And received the kind of reply that had me running to the mirror to see if my throat had been cut.'

'Ha-ha, very funny,' Jemma jeered and turned a cool face on Trina. 'I hope you told him to get lost,' she said.

'Me?' her flatmate squeaked. 'Why should I tell him to get lost? He's not my problem! Although...' she added with a teasing glance at Frew '...hearing that gorgeous sexy voice purring down the line at me had me thinking it would be quite something to have him as a problem.'

'He'd eat you for breakfast and not even notice,' Frew scoffed, refusing to rise to the bait.

'If he could eat me, what do you think he could do to Jemma?'

'Excuse me if I leave you to discuss me while I go to bed,' Jemma put in sarcastically. 'But please do continue none the less.'

'He's back in London!' Trina called as Jemma turned to leave the room. Her spine began to tingle, as though just knowing he was in the same city was enough to make her flesh respond to him. 'And he was not happy when I told him you were out on a date!'

'When I answered the phone on his last call,' Frew tagged on, 'he mistook me for your date and actually threatened to come around here and eject me!'

'I do hope you put him right,' Jemma drawled, turning to send Frew a deriding look. 'Only I would hate him to have the wrong impression about my taste!'

'Whoa there, tiger!' Trina warned. 'That's the love of my life you're insulting!'

'Well, tell the love of your damned life to keep his nose out of my business!' Jemma snapped, wondering helplessly where all that lovely relaxed contentment she had rediscovered tonight had gone.

The phone began to ring. She stiffened up like a board. So did the other two, watching her with curious eyes.

'Want me to answer it?' Trina offered gently.

Oh, yes! Jemma thought frantically. Please yes! Anyone but me! I just can't let myself be—— 'No,' she heard herself mumble gruffly. 'I'll do it.'

She walked into the kitchen and stared at the wall set for all of ten seconds before slowly lifting off the receiver.

'Jemma?'

She closed her eyes, swallowing thickly because just the sound of her name on his lips sent her mouth dry. 'Yes,' she whispered.

There was a short, very telling silence, and it didn't take much to sense the anger simmering within it. 'I want to see you,' he said tightly.

'Well, I don't——'

'Now.' Arrogantly, he cut right through her attempted refusal. 'I shall be around to collect you in half an hour.'

'But it's eleven-thirty!' she protested. 'I don't——!'

'I will sound my car horn when I arrive,' he interrupted yet again. 'You have three minutes from that moment to get in the car or I shall come up—do you understand me, Jemma?' he persisted. 'I am a man who does not play games—any kind of game.'

The line went dead. Jemma stared at it. He had just threatened her. He had actually had the gall to threaten her!

CHAPTER THREE

LEON didn't need to sound his car horn. Jemma was already waiting outside, huddled in her pale blue wool duffel-coat and simmering with resentment when the sleek silver-grey Mercedes drew up beside her.

She had a brief glimpse of his dark, chiselled features when the lamplight caught his face as he leaned across the luxurious interior to open the door for her.

He was angry, tight with it.

Well, she thought indignantly, so am I! And refused to so much as look at him as she climbed into the car and stared coldly at the windscreen.

'Seatbelt,' he snapped.

She opened her mouth to tell him to get lost, then shut it again on an inward gasp as the car shot forward on an angry burst of power. Fumbling, she fastened the belt around her, having to drop her purse and the small plastic carrier bag she had brought with her on to the car floor to do it.

Pausing at the next junction, he turned his dark head to slash her with an icy look; she gave it back defiantly, but just allowing her eyes to clash with his was enough to set her trembling, and it was he who broke the hostile contact. She had not been able to, he affected her so badly.

This is crazy, she told herself as they joined the late rush of traffic crowding the London streets. How could she be so acutely aware of a man she barely knew?

Perhaps Trina was right after all, and she had been heading for this kind of emotional fall-out for years,

33

bottling it all up, refusing to acknowledge that she had the ability to feel this way.

Trying to smother a helpless sigh, she obviously wasn't very successful, because the black eyes raked her again. She felt their touch all the way down to her toes. Don't, she wanted to say. Don't look at me—don't do this to me! But she pressed her trembling lips together and stared fixedly ahead, and after a moment he returned his attention to the road while the tension surrounding them grew so tight she could barely breathe.

He turned into a quiet, salubrious square that she recognised instantly, and a wry smile touched her mouth. Big-league wasn't in it; this man existed on a higher plane altogether than she could ever aspire to.

Good, she thought. It only helped to shore up her resolve to get out of this situation before it became impossible. She didn't want this—it—him. She did not need it, nor could she cope with it.

The car stopped, the engine dying. Leon unclipped both seatbelts then opened his car door. She watched balefully as he climbed out and came around to open her door. When she hesitated, he said coolly, 'Don't make the mistake of challenging me, Jemma. I am tired and my temper is worn thin. I could get nasty.'

Could? If he thought he was making this a pleasure then she did not want to be around when he did get 'nasty'! Bending, she scooped up her purse and the small plastic carrier bag, then slid out of the car, scorning the outstretched hand he offered her in assistance.

He closed the car door, pressed a sensor pad on his keyring which activated the car central-locking system and the alarm at the same time, then turned without sparing her another glance to climb the steps to a black-painted front door.

By the time she had joined him, he was standing inside an elegant hallway. The plain grey-carpeted floor and pale peach-painted walls blended superbly with the rich mahogany woodwork.

He glanced at a silver tray on the hall table where a stack of envelopes lay unopened. Long fingers flicked idly at them then dismissed them as unimportant. It was only then that it hit her that he must not have been here since his return to London.

So, where had he been? Working in his office? Eating dinner at some exclusive restaurant? With another woman?

Jealousy swirled up from the pit of her stomach and burned its way into her brain. Shocked and appalled by her own reaction, she stumbled as she tried to turn and walk out of the house again before he saw what was happening to her.

But Leon was too quick, and in one stride was at her side, his hand like a clamp around her arm as he turned her back again.

'Going somewhere?' he enquired silkily.

'I don't want to come in here with you,' she objected, having now to fight her response to his heated touch as well the crazy jealousy.

For an answer, he reached over her shoulder and gave the door a shove. Jemma quivered as she heard it click shut behind her. Without a single word, he took her purse and the silly plastic carrier bag from her, unbuttoned her coat and drew it off her shoulders while she just stood there in front of him, cheeks hot, eyes lowered, trembling from head to toe at his domineering closeness.

Then he just turned and walked off down the hall, arrogantly taking her possessions with him.

It's getting worse, she noted tremulously as she meekly followed. Ten minutes in his company last time and her senses had been so responsive to him that she could barely breathe or think. Another ten minutes and she was now so acutely conscious of him that she was actually afraid.

She paused on the threshold of a beautiful pale lemon and white sitting-room, seeing her coat casually discarded on the back of a chair. Leon was standing across the room, pouring a drink into a fine crystal glass, his dark business suit moulding his muscled body with little attempt at hiding the power beneath.

Her stillness had him glancing around at her. 'Come in,' he drawled. 'I am in no mood to jump on you if that is what is making you hover like a frightened bird.'

She still didn't move, her eyes too big in her face as she continued to stand there staring helplessly at him, her loose hair flowing like liquid toffee around her face and shoulders. His thick lashes lowered, half hiding his eyes while he let them travel slowly over her, lighting candles inside her wherever his gaze touched. She was still wearing the cool blue slinky stretch Lycra dress she had worn for her date with Tom. It lay off the shoulder and moulded her figure to halfway down her slender thighs. It wasn't a cheap dress, but neither was it of the expensive designer kind he was probably used to seeing his women in. And where with Tom she had only felt pretty, with Leon's eyes on her she felt vulnerable and self-conscious beneath his connoisseur's gaze.

'You dressed for him like this tonight?'

The question startled her, putting a wary light into her eyes, but it also served to remind her of why she was here at all, and Jemma lifted her chin, her mouth firming as she looked back at him.

'Yes,' she said, adding defiantly, 'not that it's any of your business.'

'No?' The smile on his lips held no humour, nor did the mocking tone. 'You have a lot to learn, if you truly believe what you say.'

He turned, gathering up another glass and bringing it with him as he walked towards her. Jemma held her ground, but only on the outside. Inside she was a broiling mass of panic. If he touched her—if he so much as laid a finger on her—she had a fear she would go up in flames.

'Here.' He held out the glass. 'Drink this.'

She looked down at the dark golden liquid gleaming in the glass. 'What is it?' she asked suspiciously.

'The national drink of Greece,' he replied. 'Come——' He gestured with the glass. 'I drink the same, so you can be assured it is not drugged. Try it. It is called metaxa—a carefully matured brandy that is kind to the palate.'

She took the glass reluctantly, lifting it to her lips to take a wary sip. Like brandy, it heated the sensitive tissues of her mouth as it flowed across it, but, unlike brandy, it did not burn. She swallowed. 'It's nice,' she allowed, sounding surprised.

He smiled, a brief smile that had gone as soon as it had arrived. Then he was staring at her again, the anger she had sensed simmering in him when he'd spoken on the phone still burning in his eyes.

'You—care for him?' he asked. 'You want this man you went out with tonight?'

'How can I say?' she cried, objecting to his proprietorial tone. 'It was our first date! Far too soon to make a decision like that!'

'Yet you knew you wanted me at the first clash of our eyes,' he pointed out.

She shrugged, unable to deny what had to be the biggest humiliation of her life. 'Which doesn't mean I have to jump right into bed with you,' she snapped. 'Wanting and having are two completely different things.'

'I am here.' He held out his arms, mocking her reply and inviting her at the same time. But she wasn't fooled; the anger was still there in his eyes. 'For the—having. Yet you decide to play this—little game with your fresh-faced young man with the winsome smile and thatch of light brown spiky hair.'

Shocked by his accurate description of Tom, she stared at him. 'How do you know what Tom looks like?' she gasped.

He took a sip at his drink, dark eyes thoughtful on her while he took his time swallowing. Her head began to spin, that awful track of uncontrollable attraction spiralling its way through her system. It was the eyes that did it, she acknowledged hazily, feeling her breath begin to shorten and her body begin to pulse to a rhythm that was strange to her yet unbearably exciting. Those deep, dark, beautiful eyes could hold her captive at a single look.

'Thomas MacDonald,' he said suddenly, bringing her sharply back into focus. 'Aged twenty-nine. Recently employed by Driver and Lowe, architects.' Jemma's mouth fell open. 'Moved into the flat below your own on Tuesday last week. Has a passion for Simply Red and never misses a concert if he can help it. His current bank account rests at one thousand and fifty-two pounds. He caught the bus to work with you on Wednesday. Borrowed teabags from your enchanting flatmate Trina Beaton on Thursday. Trina Beaton...' He moved on while Jemma could only stand there gaping. 'A delightfully enterprising creature with bright red hair and a—satirical disposition. You have shared a flat with her since you arrived in London four years ago. She runs an interesting little business called—Maids in Waiting.' He actually smiled with amusement at that. 'An idea which began during her college years in an effort to make some extra money to prop up her grant and grew into the flourishing business it is today because she had the courage and foresight to see its potential. Her accountant is also her lover—though they never use your flat for their—intimate activities—reputedly in respect of your... finer feelings. His name is Frew Landers and he's clever and sharp. Upwardly mobile, I think is the popular term. His favourite pastime is teasing you.

Jemma Davis,' he continued levelly, never for one second taking his eyes from her stunned face. 'Parents dead, killed in an automobile accident four years ago. Attended secretarial college for two yours and graduated with distinctions at the age of nineteen. Has worked for three companies, TDC being the last and current one. Josh Tanner employed you—not particularly for your exemplary secretarial skills, but because he wanted to take you to bed. But—and I compliment you on your good sense—you made him see the error of his—judgement. Since then you have become his right-hand man, though he does not realise it himself. And his complicated love-life has hit the doldrums—how is Cassie, by the way?' he concluded lightly.

'I n-need to sit d-down,' Jemma said weakly.

'Of course,' he said, immediately the indulgent host and taking her arm to lead her over to one of the comfortable damask sofas set before the flower-filled grate of a beautiful mahogany fireplace.

She lowered herself carefully, aware that the slightest puff of wind was likely to toss her into a crumpled heap. He watched her sink into a corner, her face gone quite blank, then sat himself down beside her. She was still holding her glass, and he gently curled his own fingers around it and lifted it to her ice-cold lips.

'I'm sorry,' he murmured, watching the colour take its time returning to her face. 'But you made me very angry or I would not have said any of that.'

'Why?' she managed to enunciate, but only just. In truth, he had completely knocked the stuffing out of her.

'I want you,' he shrugged as if that explained everything. 'By necessity I have to be a careful man. Power makes you dangerous, and your enemies do not always wear intentions on their sleeves. Danger can come in many guises—hostile take-overs, industrial espionage——'

'And you suspect me of being some kind of Mata Hari trained to seduce you for all your powerful secrets?' she gasped, disbelief and scorn warring in her anger-bright eyes.

He smiled, unrepentant. 'Or just a lady,' he suggested, 'with the kind of past that could affect me?'

'My God! You arrogant swine!' she choked, not for one second missing his meaning. Furiously, she shot to her feet. 'Well, hear this, Mr Stephanades,' she flung at him. 'This lady with a past is just a bit choosy herself!'

'I know,' he confirmed, his lazy smile enough to shoot the lid right off her temper.

'Oh, go to hell,' she muttered, and turned, her trembling legs barely able to support her as she stalked angrily for the door.

'Virgin,' he chanted cruelly after her. 'And proud of it. Friends call you "one-date Jemma" and lay bets on who will be the first to crack the ice.' She stopped, her spine stiffening in horror. 'Speculation has it that you must have suffered a bad experience at some time to make you so unresponsive to men. But I know better, do I not?'

Jemma closed her eyes, appalled that his investigators could dig that deep!

'I am not a promiscuous man, *agape mou*,' he informed her smoothly. 'The days of passing from one woman to another long ago lost its appeal with the risks it brings with it. I value my good clean bill of health, and am therefore very careful whom I share my body with.'

'My God,' she whispered, turning to stare at him. 'I don't believe I'm really hearing this!'

'I want you, but not at any price—you understand?' he said, a slight hint of apology in his tone as he came to his feet. 'So I had to have you thoroughly checked out.'

'So virgins are all you allow yourself these days, are they?' Jemma threw scathingly at him.

His open-palmed shrug said it all. 'In general, these days, I steer clear of intimacy with any women,' he confessed. 'You, are the exception.'

'And I suppose you expect me to be honoured by that confession?'

'No,' he denied. 'But I thought you may gain some comfort in knowing that I can offer you the same risk-free pleasure you will be giving me.'

'Go to hell,' she said again, her contempt of him only slightly overshadowed by the severe sense of disgust she felt at herself for being so obvious with him that he felt he could do and say all of this to her. 'I would rather take my chances with Tom MacDonald's more dubious sexual history than with a cold-blooded, calculating devil like you!'

On that, she spun away again, grabbing up her belongings before storming out of the room, feeling angry enough just maybe to put her words into practice and offer herself to Tom, if only to get back at all of them— both her so-called friends and the man she had just left standing there—for daring to make her personal life their business!

She'd reached the front door before he caught up with her, his hands like manacles as they closed around her upper arms to swing her round to face him. Her coat went one way, her purse the other. She saw the fury leaping in his eyes, the threat of violence, then his mouth was landing punishingly on hers and all hell broke loose inside her.

Her shock, the anger and utter contempt she was feeling, all colluded with her hungry senses to send them wild. Her arms snapped up to push him away, fists thumping at his shoulders and chest while she wriggled and squirmed and kissed him back with a vengeance. Her lips parted, wantonly drawing his tongue into contest with her own, and he made a husky little groan deep in his throat which she answered with an animal growl of her own, elated that she had actually managed to shake him.

'You think I would let you give all of this to him?' he grated, thrusting her to arm's length so that she fell heavily against the hard wood panel of the door behind her.

'Good, was it?' she taunted thickly, her eyes spitting her contempt at him, even while her swollen mouth invited more of the same mind-blowing kisses. Breasts heaving, hands shaking, she challenged the harsh rasping of his breath. 'Want it all? Shame,' she jeered. 'Because I'd die before I would let you have me!'

'Then die!' he decreed, dragging her back against him, the desire in him flaring up like her own, full of angry passion. 'For I am the only man who is going to have you!'

And his mouth took hers again, his arms moulding her writhing throbbing body to his with no chance of escape. And it went on and on—a battle that was a crazy one because they were both using the same angry weapons to strike sparks from each other. Jemma's fingers found his hair and gripped, but not to pull him away. Instead they held his mouth down on hers while his own hands curved into the flesh at the tops of her legs, pushing up the fabric of her skirt and pressing her hard against him so that the mad gyration of their bodies inflamed them to full, throbbing arousal.

It was terrible. Jemma saw in a brief flash of sanity how they must look together like this, and she whimpered in horror, hot tears burning into her eyes and running down her cheeks.

He felt them, tasted them on his tongue, and groaned as he dragged his mouth away from hers. 'God,' he choked, 'what are we doing here?'

Raping each other, Jemma thought wildly as he muttered something in a harsh guttural Greek before burying his face in her hair, holding her tightly against him while the wild storm raged on inside them both.

It was a long while before they began to calm. And by then Jemma was feeling so ashamed of herself that she did not know how she was going to lift her head and face him. She was glad of the solid wall of his pounding chest to hide against. His arms had relaxed their suffocating grip on her body and were gently stroking her now. He, like herself, made no attempt to move, but slowly, as the seconds ticked by, she became conscious that one of them was going to have to break the crazy deadlock.

He did it, as if reading her mind, taking on the responsibility and slowly dropping his arms. She didn't move, didn't think she had the strength left to try! He turned his back, a hand going up to grip the back of his neck while he stared grimly at the carpet. The silence was gnawing.

'I'll make some coffee,' he said suddenly and strode off down the hall.

Jemma watched him go with empty eyes. Empty because he had just managed to drain her of every emotion she possessed. It would be better if she just opened the door and sneaked quietly away, she told herself as she continued to stand there. She was sure she would be able to hail a cruising black cab. Ten minutes and she would be home, safe in her flat with Trina's mocking presence to keep her safe. A few determined steps, she told herself, and you could end all of this for good. He would not follow. Like herself, he couldn't want this violent kind of passion.

It wasn't good. It wasn't even enjoyable. Just a hostile, bitter slaking of an ugly lust, that was what it was. Lust.

She managed to turn, legs trembling as she made the vital manoeuvre which had her facing the door.

'Where are you going?'

Gentle as the question was, it froze her in terror. 'H-home,' she whispered tremulously. 'I w-want to go h-home.'

Silence. She didn't move and she was almost sure he didn't either. Then she heard his heavy sigh. 'All right,' he conceded. 'But I shall take you.'

He began walking towards her, and the closer he got, the more she trembled until she shook in violent spasms that brought the tears back to her eyes. It was stupid, but when his arms came gently around her to draw her back against him she sobbed with relief, turning to bury her face in his shirt-front. 'I've never felt so ashamed of myself!' she whispered thickly.

'You and me both, *agape mou*,' he murmured grimly. 'But I think my shame has to be worse than yours right now. Come.' He shifted until he held her beneath the crook of his arm. 'You are in no fit state to go home as yet, and my guilty conscience will not let you go like this.' Gently he led her back along the hall. 'We will talk, I think,' he decided. 'Of things other than ourselves and what we seem to want or not want.' His dry tone made her smile, and she glanced up to find him smiling ruefully too.

Then their eyes locked. And even as she felt the upward surge of all that awful tension again, she saw him heave in a harsh breath in an effort to control his own feelings.

Sighing, he leaned back heavily against the wall behind him, his grip loosening on her. 'This is not going to work, is it?' he sighed. 'Talking is the last thing we both need to do right now.'

She lowered her face, shaking her tumbled mass of hair. 'I don't even know you,' she whispered helplessly. That seemed to shame her as much as the emotions running wild inside her.

'Our bodies seem to know each other well enough.' Reaching out, he threaded gentle fingers through her hair. Her eyes closed, face lifting on a sigh of such helpless pleasure at his touch that he breathed once, fiercely. 'Upstairs,' he murmured, 'I have a bed. A warm and comfortable, very large bed where, with a bit of trust on your side and a lot of control on mine, I think I could manage to salvage some of our self-respect from this night if you would let me.'

Her stomach muscles contracted, sending a flutter of appeal winging out across her body. 'Violence is not my way, Jemma,' he said quietly. 'What took place here just now was a—a culmination of my bad temper and your angry retaliation to it. But it does not alter the most fundamental reason as to why we are here together like this. We want each other—*need* would be a better word. Please,' he murmured huskily, 'will you let me make love to you as gently and as beautifully as I know how?'

'No strings attached?' She heard the words leave her lips in the shape of a surrender, her kiss-swollen mouth twisting wryly as she acknowledged it. 'No other lovers? No other commitment other than a pledge of loyalty while this thing lasts?' she quoted his own words back at him drily.

'Do you want a deeper commitment from me?' he asked, his expression quite serious.

Jemma thought about it. Thought about the man he was and the power he wielded. She thought about the social circles he moved in and the nice little Greek girl at home somewhere in his own country waiting for him to give in to family pressure and marry well. And she shuddered. 'No,' she answered. 'I want nothing more from you than—this...'

She moved into his arms, unable to stay out of them for a moment longer. Their mouths met and her eyes closed over the helpless need radiating from her dark blue irises. Leon came away from the wall, folding her against him as he deepened the kiss.

The anger had gone, lost in the surrendering of the battle. But what replaced it was far, far more intense. With the aid of his kiss he seemed to absorb her into him, her mind, her body, her every sense opening up and closing hungrily around him.

He whispered something, a stunned expletive, it sounded like, though she barely registered it because whatever it was was groaned against her burning mouth and she was more aware of him picking her up and cradling her in his arms then moving, carrying her in a floaty haze up the stairs.

The kiss broke when he lowered her feet to the ground again, and Jemma lifted heavy lids to find herself gazing into eyes flowing with passion. It startled her, the look of fierce arousal, and her mouth parted on a protest—never uttered because he stopped it with a small shake of his head.

'Trust me,' he said, brushing his lips across hers. 'This is no empty seduction. I am as much a slave to this as you are, *agape mou*.'

A statement he quickly proved when her fingers flexed in an instinctive response against his shoulders and he shuddered, the breath rushing shakily from his lungs.

Taking hold of her hand, he led her across the room—a room, she realised for the first time, that was a bedroom, big and gracious, its green and grey furnishings softly lit by a bedside lamp.

By the big double bed he turned her to face him, eyes still black with need but gentle now as they gravely explored her face. She blushed, feeling shy suddenly and awkward now that he had given her a moment to realise just what they were doing.

'No,' he murmured, lifting her chin with softly stroking fingers when she tried to hide her face from him. 'Passion becomes you, *agape mou*. Don't hide it all away from me.'

He lowered his head again, silk lashes brushing tantilisingly against her flushed cheeks as he kissed her nose then each corner of her mouth and ran his fingers in a feather-like caress down her throat and over naked shoulders before sliding them into her hair, pushing the long, thick fall back from her face and making her senses leap as he lowered his head to run his tongue around her exposed ear.

She closed her eyes, preening sensually as the sweetest sensation turned her muscles to liquid. Her fingers curled into the lean, tight flesh at his waist. His tongue slid lower, forcing the breath from her lungs in short, sharp gasps as he licked his way to the other ear to wreak the same havoc there.

Then his mouth closed over hers again, his hands sliding down the sides of her body from breast to hip and back again, sending her arching sensuously towards him as, slowly, he began peeling her dress downwards. It had no zip, was nothing more than a tube of stretch fabric and it went easily, exposing her breasts, high-domed and peaked by two tight buds. His hands explored, probed, excited, then pushed the dress further, over her slender ribcage, her narrow waist and the softly rounded curves of her hips. By the time it fell in a pool around her feet, her arms were curved languidly around his neck, all hint of shyness lost to the pleasure of his touch.

They were kissing so deeply now that she was barely aware of his quick movements as he divested himself of his shirt. It was only as he crushed her against the heat of his naked chest that she realised what he had done. And by then she was revelling in the feel of him, of the hard-packed muscle beneath heated flesh, his skin like stretched satin beneath her fingertips, of the rasping pleasure of chest hair moving against her breast. The scent of him was warm and clean and intoxicatingly musky, sensual, so sensual that it sent her dizzy, dizzy

enough to sigh and sway, and groan something helpless
in her throat which she didn't understand but he seemed
to do because he turned and, with her still held in his
arms, lowered them both on to the cool green cover on
the bed.

It was a long night. A beautiful night. Tender and
excruciatingly patient, Leon guided her down sweet,
sweet paths of sensual pleasure. He taught her with each
new intimacy what making love really meant. First of
the flesh, bringing her skin alive with the lightest, most
tantalising caresses until she seemed to quiver all over
with a bright tingling pleasure that had her arching and
flexing in movements that were so instinctively sensual
that she had no idea what it did to him to feel her like
this.

But she thought she'd die a thousand deaths at the
confusing rush of feeling she felt when his touch became
more intimate.

'Shh,' he soothed as she tightened in shocked rejection to something utterly alien to her, and he caught
her shaky protest with his mouth while his fingers stroked
the moist, silken core of her, drawing her—inexorably
drawing her—deeper into the chasms of desire.

It flowed and ebbed, like a lazy summer tide washing
over her until she thought she would drown in its sensual
flow, only to feel it fade away again as, skilfully, she
realised hazily, he brought her to a boneless state where
nothing he could do would shock her now. She began
to feel restless, her body pulsing to a rhythm that seemed
to demand something more from him.

'Leon,' she whispered threadily.

'Yes,' he murmured. 'I know...' And he took her
mouth in a long, languid kiss while gently urging her
thighs wider, then slid his body over hers.

No pain, just a short, sharp sting that had her eyes
flying open on a breathless, 'Oh,' to stare at him
in surprise.

He was watching her, supporting his upper body on his forearms as he gazed into her eyes, his own face wearing the glaze of a fiercely reined-in passion. He was hot and tight, his laboured breath rasping over her face as he waited, lean hips pressing into the cradle of her hips, letting her feel—know—the power of his possession before slowly, carefully he thrust himself deeper inside.

Then they were one, moving together, breathing together. Mouths locked, bodies locked, and the pounding drumbeat of their hearts paced the growing power of their pleasure. She could feel him inside her, exalted in his pulsing strength, the power of him, the need in him, each stroke, each beautiful silken stroke carrying them closer and closer to some potent place hovering just out of their grasp.

Then suddenly they reached it, and as if a volcano were erupting deep inside her she was tossed into a world of fire and force and hot, pulsing lava.

Afterwards she curled herself up into his arms, clinging to him as though life itself revolved around him in its entirety. The fact that he held her close, said nothing but just held her, told her that he too was in awe of what had just happened. She hadn't expected it; she wondered if he had.

Whatever. As far as she was concerned, Leon had just given her the most beautiful experience of her life, and at this moment she wanted to do nothing more than be held close to him while she savoured it. Because surely it could not be that good every time, could it?

CHAPTER FOUR

'ARE you going to move in with him?' Trina demanded. It was late Sunday night and Jemma had not returned until half an hour ago.

What had gone on in the interim would, Jemma thought dreamily, go down in her secret store of memories as the most precious forty-eight hours of her life. As he had promised, Leon had made that first time beautiful for her. His care and patience and mind-blowing sensuality had left her stunned and dazed.

And it could be as good the second and even the third time around, she acknowledged with a soft secret smile. In fact, their responses to each other became so exquisitely tuned that they could barely look at each other without experiencing the electric fizz of desire.

'No,' she answered Trina's question, then grimaced, remembering the one of several small skirmishes they'd had during the weekend. 'He wants me to, but I decided it was best if I remain here. I'll find it less—stressful that way. He goes away a lot, and that big empty house would drive me insane with no one to talk to.'

'No servants?'

She shook her head. 'A woman who comes in daily to clean for him, but nothing more. If he wishes to entertain, he employs a caterer. He is surprisingly self-sufficient for someone from his background,' she confided with a smile. 'And his tastes are simple.'

'A Greek trait,' he'd told her. 'At heart all Greeks are simple people. We make money by necessity—and because we find we possess a rather good knack for doing so,' he'd added with a grin. 'But I live in a world constantly filled with people. People who are in constant demand of my attention, my thoughts, my time. When I come home I want only to answer to myself. Servants fussing around me would spoil that.'

'And so would a lover,' she'd pointed out. 'So I am right to remain in my own flat.'

He'd frowned at her when she'd said that, as if he wanted to argue—then changed his mind, pulling her towards him and kissing the top of her head. 'Perhaps you are at that,' he'd agreed. 'Except the weekends,' he'd added firmly, 'when you will arrive here directly from work on Friday and remain until Sunday night. And I will buy you a wardrobe of exquisite clothes so you won't have to waste time packing and unpacking.'

Which had begun the next small skirmish—or maybe it wasn't so small, she mused as she sat there on the lumpy old sofa after enjoying a day of sinking into luxurious feather.

'No wardrobe,' she'd refused. 'And no more presents, Leon,' she'd added, going to dig out the reason she had actually decided to meet him the night before, and handing the plastic carrier bag to him. 'You take me as I am—nine-carat-gold jewellery, off-the-peg clothes and all—or not at all, but I don't want any more...gifts.'

He stared down at the plastic bag for a moment before silently opening it up. Out fell the velvet boxes.

'I don't want you to buy me things,' she explained huskily when he didn't say a single word. 'When you do, it makes me feel...' She paused, searching for the right word which wouldn't offend.

He provided it. 'Cheap?' he clipped.

'Inadequate,' she amended. 'I can't match your generosity, Leon, simply because I don't have the necessary funds to do it. When you buy me expensive things, it makes me feel...'

'Bought.'

'Will you stop putting words into my mouth?' she flared, irritated because really he was only stating the truth. 'You are deliberately misconstruing everything I say!'

'And you are not misconstruing my reason for buying you these things?' he countered, suddenly so contemptuous that it hit her that she had managed to offend him anyway. 'You call these expensive!' On an act of disgust he threw the boxes to one side. 'They were nothing but *cheap* little nothings I saw and bought for you because they pleased my eye and reminded me of you!'

She gasped at the interpretation he had put on her words. 'So your choice of word was right, and I do look cheap?' she retaliated, her own anger and hurt rising with his.

'If you looked cheap, my dear Jemma,' he decided, 'you would not be standing here in my home right now!'

'So, why are you offering to buy me an expensive wardrobe of clothes?' she challenged. 'Why the expensive—sorry, *cheap* gifts? If it offends your ego to be with a woman who wears high-street bargain clothes and gold-plated jewellery, Leon, then maybe we should just call it quits right now!'

'I never said that!' he sighed in exasperation. 'Or even implied it! You are a very beautiful woman, Jemma—sackcloth or silk, you would always look beautiful. Why is it so wrong for a man to want to buy his woman beautiful things?'

'Because this particular woman feels more comfortable without them,' she replied. 'I have nothing but myself to give to you and I want nothing but yourself in return. Is that so difficult to understand?' she appealed.

He sighed at that, and, in a way which brought tears to her eyes, reached out and drew her against him. 'You are wrong, you know,' he murmured into her hair. 'You have given me the most expensive and precious gift a woman can give a man, *agape mou*. And if I let it pass by unacknowledged, then I would certainly be playing you cheap.'

She blushed, knowing exactly what he was referring to. 'It was given freely, Leon,' she whispered softly.

'And cannot be handed back as my—paltry gifts to you can be,' he pointed out.

She lifted her head to look at him at that, her eyes suddenly alight with mischief. 'And do you want to give it back?' she enquired provocatively.

'Vixen,' he scolded. 'You know I do not! But,' he added, 'in all fairness, according to your rules, you must accept something back from me in return.'

'All right,' she reluctantly conceded. 'One gift I will accept graciously—but nothing else!' she warned him sternly. 'And something small! If I come here next Friday night to find a wardrobe stuffed with fine clothes, I'll throw them out of the window!'

'Jemma...?'

'Mmm?' she murmured hazily now, the tender smile softening her face taking its time to fade as she slowly refocused.

Trina was looking anxious. 'Are you absolutely sure you're doing the right thing?'

No, Jemma thought, but I know I can't do a thing about it. She got up, stretching tiredly. 'What's right or wrong for me doesn't seem to come into it,' she confessed as she let her body relax again. 'I want him,' she tagged on simply. It seemed to say it all to her.

'You love him, you mean,' Trina grimly corrected.

Did she? Jemma paused to ponder a concept she had until now refused to so much as peep at. Had she fallen head over heels in love with Leon Stephanades at the first moment she saw him?

'I know you, Jemma, and there's no way you would put yourself in this kind of no-hope situation unless your heart was involved. You love him,' she stated again. 'And that bastard most probably knows it, and couldn't give a hoot so long as he gets what he wants from you!'

'I'm going to bed,' Jemma said pointedly, turning towards the door. 'Goodnight, Tri.'

'He'll hurt you!' her friend warned, real concern darkening her rich green eyes. 'He's the kind of man who sees something he wants and goes after it and damns the consequences! It wouldn't enter his arrogant head to wonder whether it was the right and fair thing for you! Men like him exist on a different plane from us mere mortals. They're takers, Jemma!'

'And you think I'm not taking as much from him?' she challenged.

'It's not the same,' Trina sighed. 'You'll be the one left hurting in the end while he walks away sublimely unscathed! Oh,' she groaned in frustration when she saw Jemma's set face. 'Why couldn't you have put it around a bit like the rest of us more normal creatures? Gained some experience before taking on a man like him!'

'Goodnight, Trina,' Jemma sighed out wearily, announcing the end of the discussion.

'Goodnight,' her friend mumbled. Then, as Jemma reached the door, 'I hate him!' she yelled at the top of her voice.

'I'll be sure to tell him,' Jemma replied, smiling, because poor Trina was only behaving like this out of concern for her.

'You won't need to,' Trina snapped, 'because I'll damn well tell him myself!'

And she did.

It was Wednesday before Jemma saw Leon again. He was tied up with business until then, and in a way Jemma was glad of the respite. Not least because her body physically ached from the sensual onslaught it had been put through.

He called her at work, though. Usually around three each afternoon, his voice like warm honey on her senses, gliding sweetly over her. On Wednesday, she received a beautiful posy of freesias, their luxurious scent filling the whole office. 'Not a gift,' he'd sardonically written on the accompanying card, 'but a hello because I will not have time to call you today. And I wanted to remind you to keep tonight free. It belongs to me. L.'

She smiled at his sarcasm, grimaced at his arrogance and inhaled the lovely perfume of the flowers as if she were inhaling that subtle spicy scent of him.

'Who's L?'

She hadn't heard Josh come in the room, and jumped when she found him leaning over her, blatantly reading the card. 'An—admirer,' she said, and quickly shoved the card away. She didn't want Josh to know about Leon. Things between the two men were strained enough as it was.

Cassie, it seemed, had gone into hiding. And Josh, for all he tried, could not find out where she was and was therefore blaming Leon. 'The man's no fool, I'll give him that!' Josh had grated bitterly after spending hours trying to locate Cassie. 'If she's with him then he's managed to secure himself the safest lay in town!'

'Josh!' Jemma had gasped. 'That's a terrible thing to say!'

He'd muttered something beneath his breath, scraped an angry hand through his straight blond hair then stormed back into his own room.

When Leon picked her up on Wednesday night, her first question was, 'Have you seen Cassie?'

His frown was genuine enough. 'No,' he said. 'Why should I? Aren't you ready?' he then demanded impatiently, glancing at her white towelling robe than pointedly at his watch, poor Cassie firmly dismissed. 'The table is booked for eight. I dislike being late.'

Reassured about Cassie, Jemma then forgot all about her when another concern leapt into her mind. The one which meant leaving him alone with Trina while she finished getting ready.

By the time she joined them, you could have cut the air with a knife. Leon was standing by the window, his elegant back in its beautifully cut dark silk suit an arrogant wall of dismissal. Trina was seated hot-faced on the sofa, glaring fiery daggers at him. Jemma took one look at them both and bit down anxiously on her bottom lip. Leon was a sophisticated man of the world, and not the kind you gave moral lectures to. She didn't want Trina spoiling this for her.

'I'm ready,' she murmured nervously.

He turned, his eyes darkening as they ran over her. She was wearing black tonight, figure-hugging silk jacquard black with a halter-neck that left her shoulders bare and fastened like a dog-collar around her slender neck. It was fashionably short, revealing more than enough of her long, slender legs. And she'd put up her hair, tying it in a topknot then teasing down some wispy tendrils to soften the shape of her face.

She knew she looked good. But under his expert eye she was severely on the look-out for any hint of criticism. What she actually saw made her blush warmly as she turned away to collect her bag, only remembering what the back of the dress did when she heard his indrawn gasp.

In fact, the dress did not have a back. It hugged her breasts and skimmed down the sides of her ribcage to her waist, but other than that she was naked.

'Want to borrow my black wrap?' Trina offered in an odd tone of voice which had her glancing sharply at her. It was then she realised that the offer had not been made out of the goodness of her heart, but as a taunt to the man who was staring at Jemma in a way that increased her anxiety. Had she gone too far? Was the dress too revealing for his taste?

'Do you think I need one?' She put the question to Leon—and they all knew she was not referring to the unusually warm weather they were having for April.

'He thinks you need bedding,' Trina drawled. 'But that is beside the——'

'Shut up, you acid-tongued bitch,' Leon cut in levelly. He didn't even flash Trina a threatening glance when he said it, just relayed the words with a cool indifference that made Trina shrug and Jemma gasp. 'You'll do exactly as you are,' he then murmured to Jemma. And the tone alone showed the perfect example of what a voice could say without using the right words.

She was still trembling with reaction to it when he opened the sitting-room door and politely saw her through it.

'Wait a minute,' Leon stalled her as she went to walk down the narrow hall.

She turned, lifting a self-conscious hand to her hair when she found him studying her narrowly. 'What is it?' she asked worriedly.

'Come here,' he commanded, 'and I will show you.' She went to stand nervously in front of him.

His hands came to her waist, almost managing to span the slender width as he drew her against him. 'She's right, you know,' he murmured huskily. 'I do want to bed you.'

His mouth was warm and seeking, hungry, without attempting to fan the fires they both knew were being carefully banked down right now. His fingers played lightly on her naked back, setting her flesh tingling as they brushed tantalisingly over her, his thumbs finding their way inside the dress to caress the satin sides of her breasts. She arched against him in seductive pleasure, and he groaned against her mouth, their lips clinging protestingly as they slowly broke apart.

'Feel what you do to me?' he murmured.

'Mmm,' she smiled, and presented her mouth for another kiss. He was just lowering his head when the rattle of the sitting-room door broke them both apart.

'Ah,' he mocked. 'The wicked witch is about to appear.'

'She's not a witch,' Jemma protested as she put some distance between them. 'And she's not wicked. She's just concerned for me, that's all.'

'And I admire her for that,' Leon surprised her by saying as he guided her towards the flat door. 'But it does not alter the fact that she has a mind like a sewer and the tongue of an asp!'

'Does it bother you,' Jemma asked him anxiously as they reached the top of the stairs, 'that she doesn't mind saying what she thinks to your face?'

'Bother me?' An eyebrow arched sardonically. 'Of course not. She believes she has your best interests at heart.' His hand came to her nape, curving it caressingly. 'And for that reason she can snipe at me all she wants, so long as she does not succeed in convincing you that what she believes is in the truth.'

Bending his head, he kissed the tip of her nose, then smiled, and Trina was forgotten—like everything else as he set himself out to charm and amuse her throughout the long, leisurely taken dinner at the kind of restaurant Jemma had only read about in good magazines.

He drove her home to her flat afterwards.

Her body grew cold as they went way beyond the point where she could continue fooling herself that he was taking the long way back to his own home.

Was this it? she wondered achingly. Thanks for everything, Jemma, but I've decided you're not really what I want in my life?

By the time he stopped the car, she was like a statue frozen in ice in the seat beside him. She couldn't believe it—couldn't understand why, when he had been so openly warm and tender all evening. His eyes had never left her for a moment, his concentration on her alone, so intense that she'd begun to glow inside in anticipation of what was to come.

Slipping free both their seatbelts, he turned, making her jerk violently as his long-fingered hand curved around her nape again. 'Thank you,' he said. 'For a beautiful evening.'

She swallowed, unable to stand it, turning pain-glazed eyes up to his. 'Y-you don't want me tonight?' she whispered tremulously.

'Want you...?' he repeated, black eyes frowning down at her. Then he caught on and sighed heavily. 'I am not a married man, Jemma,' he derided, 'with a wife and two-point-five children at home to give me all the companionship I require.'

'I never said you were!' she protested.

'Yet you expected me to treat you as a married man treats his mistress? Seeing you—being with you—only when I need some sexual relief?'

She frowned in confusion. She'd thought that was exactly what all this was about.

Removing his hand, he sat back in his seat. 'This is supposed to be a relationship!' he snapped out impatiently. 'Not a convenience!'

'I'm sorry,' she mumbled, feeling a fool for reading the situation so terribly wrong.

'You insult me!' he claimed stiffly.

'Well!' she snapped back defensively. 'How am I supposed to know the way these things are played? It is my first try at it after all! Perhaps you had better write down the ground rules so I won't insult your sensibilities again!'

Huffily, she turned, searching for the door lock, feeling a big enough fool to want to get away from him as soon as she could.

'Come back here!' he growled, catching her by the arm and pulling her around and against him. 'You crazy woman.' His chest lifted and fell beneath her cheek on a long-suffering sigh. 'You've been sweet and amusing and downright seductive all evening.' She felt his mouth brush against her hair. 'And if I've had to fight the urge to rush you home to my bed, then I did so out of respect for you, not because I did not want you. But come Friday...' he growled, pushing her away a little so that he could burn her with his eyes. 'Pack only a toothbrush, *agape mou*. It will be all you will need for two days!'

He was right: her toothbrush was all she needed. Which from then on set the pattern for Jemma's first real love-affair. If he was in town, then Wednesday evenings they spent simply enjoying each other's company. If he was away, then each night he would ring her up and spend long delicious minutes just talking to her via the phone. Weekends he always managed to be in London, working his tight and busy schedule around it, Jemma guessed when sometimes he looked so tired when she arrived at his home on Fridays that it filled her with warmth to know he would go to such lengths just to be with her.

One Wednesday, almost a month into their relationship, he looked tired when he picked her up, and Trina's acid glances seemed to irritate him. 'I'll tell her to lay off you, shall I?' Jemma suggested when they'd driven the distance between her flat and a small but exclusive restaurant he intended taking her to in total silence.

'She does not bother me unduly,' he dismissed. 'I have been continent-hopping for the last two days, and I am just a trifle jet-lagged, that's all.'

She studied him, seeing the lines of weariness tugging at the corners of his eyes and mouth, and gently placed her hand on his thigh. 'We don't have to go anywhere if you don't feel like it, Leon,' she told him softly.

He glanced at her, mockery twisting his beautiful mouth. 'You wish me to stop here? And we'll just spend the rest of the evening in the car?'

'No.' She smiled at his sarcastic humour. 'But we could go back to your house,' she suggested. 'Spend the evening just—relaxing.'

The car slowed while he spent several seconds reading the message in her eyes before, without a word, he returned his attention to the road. He didn't say anything, but his hand came to cover hers where it rested on his thigh, and remained there until they concluded their journey to his home.

That night they made love, then she made them omelettes for supper, strolling casually about his modern kitchen wearing only one of his shirts. He sat at the kitchen table in his dark towelling robe, following her lazily with his eyes. The mood was lazy, beautifully so. After they'd eaten in front of the TV set in his sitting-room, he stretched out on the sofa and pulled her down to lie beside him. In ten minutes he was asleep.

She just lay there watching him for hours, loving the way all the toughness had left his face, how he slept with his lips slightly parted, breathing light and evenly. At twelve o'clock she crept out of the house and caught a taxi back to her flat. The next morning he rang her at work before she'd even taken off her coat.

'You left me to make your own way home,' he said. 'Don't do it again.'

'You were sleeping,' she explained. 'It wouldn't have been fair to disturb you when a taxi could transport me door to door just as easily.'

'But without the pleasure it would have given me to do so,' he stated. 'Tonight I expect reparation. Wear something sexy—like that disgraceful black thing you wore for me the first time I took you out. We are going somewhere special. I will pick you up at eight.'

The phone went dead. Jemma grinned at it. 'Arrogant devil,' she murmured, and spent the rest of the day smiling like an idiot because he was breaking from routine and taking her out on a Thursday.

Cassie rang during the afternoon. 'Will he speak to me?' she enquired stiffly.

'I'm not sure...' Jemma gave the closed door between the two offices a dubious glance. 'But I shall certainly try for you. How are you, Cassie?' she then asked gently.

'I'm fine,' came the cool reply. 'He's offered to keep me and the child, did you know that?'

Jemma mumbled a denial, hurting for both of them. Josh had not been the same person since this thing with Cassie blew up in his face. He walked around the office like a man made of stone, hard-faced and unapproachable.

'I was informed of his proposal through his solicitor,' Cassie continued tightly. 'A quarterly allowance and the mortgage taken care of on my flat.'

Jemma winced. 'I'm so sorry it worked out this way,' she murmured inadequately. In all honesty, she didn't know which of them she felt more sorry for. The whole situation was hopeless and ugly. 'If you need anything,' she offered, 'a sympathetic ear or just someone to yell at, I'm available.'

'Thanks, but no, thanks,' Cassie refused, her tone softened slightly by the offer. 'I don't think that would be a good idea.'

She meant her closeness to Josh, of course, and Jemma sighed as she buzzed him to tell him who wanted to speak to him. Surprisingly, he took the call without the bitter anger that Cassie's calls before had aroused in him.

They talked for several minutes before her console told them they'd finished. And she began to hope that, at last, tempers had calmed enough for them to begin talking sensibly about what they were going to do.

Those hopes were dashed the moment she saw Josh's face a few minutes later. He was even more stone-like than he had been before.

That evening, Leon was in a much livelier frame of mind. He even took Trina on, provoking her with teasing little remarks that ended with her stalking from the room. 'She's all fire, that one,' he remarked admiringly as he watched her go.

'Keep your eyes off!' Jemma warned. 'She's taken and so are you!'

His eyebrows shot up at her heated tone. 'That wouldn't be a hint of green-eyed jealousy, would it?' he taunted.

You can bet you sweet life it was! Jemma thought angrily, and lifted her chin. 'Do I need to feel jealous?' she challenged right back.

'Maybe,' he murmured thoughtfully. 'Red-haired witch or not, she does tend to grow on one, does she not?'

Jemma spun her back on him to collect her bag, refusing to rise to the bait. He was riling her deliberately; she knew that even as she seethed inside. Stalking haughtily out of her flat, she vowed to get her own back, if only to cut the arrogant devil down to size!

She got her opportunity sooner than she could have hoped.

Tom MacDonald was just coming out of his flat as she came down the stairs.

His face lit up when he saw her. 'Where were you the other Saturday night?' he demanded. 'I thought we had a date, but when I knocked on your flat door nobody answered!'

'Oh, Tom—I'm so sorry!' she cried, genuinely contrite because she had forgotten all about him! Impulsively, she lifted her hands to his shoulders and kissed his cheek. 'How could it have slipped my mind like that?'

'Maybe because you had other, more important things to think about,' another voice coolly suggested, and Jemma flushed with embarrassment when Leon pointedly gripped her wrists and lifted her hands away from Tom. 'Shame on you, darling,' he added smoothly, 'standing one man up while you made love to another.'

'It didn't matter,' Tom put in awkwardly, seeing more than his match in Leon and not even trying to stand up to him. 'It was only a tentative arrangement.'

'Ah,' drawled Leon. 'Then thankfully her... memory lapse did not cause too much inconvenience.' He dropped one of Jemma's wrists but held on to the other one with a grip aimed to hurt. 'You are lucky, my darling,' he murmured smoothly to her. 'Your—friend is willing to forgive your—tardiness. Other people may not be so willing.'

Now there was a threat if Jemma had ever heard one. She glowered at him, and he gazed coolly back. 'Now, say goodnight to your—friend,' he chanted softly, but his teeth were clenched tightly together while he said it. 'We are late enough as it is.'

'You're hateful!' she whispered as he pushed her in front of him and out of the house, leaving Tom staring awkwardly after them. 'How dare you tell him we were making love?'

'We were, were we not?' he challenged, wearing his arrogance like a mask on his mocking face.

She tugged at her wrist. 'Let go of me,' she demanded. 'You're hurting!'

'And if I ever see you kissing another man like that——' he turned angrily on her '—I shall hurt you a lot more!' His grip tightened for a short threatening second before he threw it away from him.

'Now who's green with jealousy?' she taunted, and gained real satisfaction from the way he stopped in the middle of opening the car door, his dark head shooting up as if her words had stabbed him in the back. Jemma stood watching him with her teeth pressing down on her bottom lip. She'd gone too far, she realised. Leon was not a man who liked his weaknesses thrown back in his face.

'Get in,' he said, and walked around to the other side of the car to climb in himself. It wasn't like him. If Leon possessed any endearing quality at all to offset his arrogance, then it had to be his impeccable manners. Always, he made sure she was inside the car and comfortable before closing the door for her.

'Where are we going?' she asked when the silence between them grew too tense for her to cope with.

'To a party,' he told her. 'It is time you met my friends.'

Oh, God, she thought heavily. That's all I need tonight—to meet his rich, sophisticated friends while he's in this mood and I feel like throttling him!

CHAPTER FIVE

THE party was in full swing when they got there, people spilling out of dimly lit rooms with glasses in their hands and false smiles on their faces. And most of them turned to stare as they walked in. She supposed Leon alone would get such a reaction, but with her by his side the interest honed in on her, and despite their mutual hostility she moved closer to him.

'I feel like a curiosity on show,' she muttered. 'This isn't Madame Tussaud's, is it?'

At least he smiled, even if she was being sarcastic. 'Too many famous faces for you?' he mocked.

'Too many something,' she agreed. 'That's Mike Williams over there, and I know for a fact that he's in Madame Tussaud's because I saw it on TV the other month!'

'Do you want me to introduce you to him?' he offered.

'No.' Jemma studied the attractive pop star from beneath her lashes. 'He isn't my type.'

'And just what is your type?' he enquired, that coolness returning to his voice.

Black-haired arrogant devils with sexy Greek accents! she thought angrily. And sighed, refusing to answer him.

'Leon, darling!' With a voice like thick syrup, the most exquisite creature Jemma had ever seen glided up to them. She was as dark as Jemma was fair and wearing white taffeta silk that shone like the five-string pearl choker she had clasped around her beautiful throat. 'You made it after all!'

Her arms went around his neck, and by the time they parted again Jemma had been effectively shoved to one side and the newcomer stood firmly in her place, her arm lovingly crooked through his. 'Carlos is here and dying to speak to you,' the woman informed him. 'That Pritchard deal you set up was an amazing coup for him! Come and...'

Jemma didn't hear any more, because the two of them had been casually swallowed up in the crowd, leaving her standing there feeling as redundant as a rag on a highly polished floor!

And that is exactly what you are! she told herself bitterly. Nothing but a rag among all these riches.

Well, 'all that glisters is not gold', she mused acidly as she let her hooded gaze scan the glittering crowd. For a start, she was sure that was Sonia Craven over there, locked in a heated clinch with a man who was most definitely not her husband.

'Been deserted?' a light male voice murmured from just behind her. She spun, and found a stranger—who was not quite a stranger because she had seen his face plastered on billboards all over the city advertising his latest film—offering her the same smile that knocked women dead all over the world. 'I saw you come in with Stephanades,' he explained his opening gambit. His incredibly piercing blue eyes slid down her then back again. 'I'll give it to him,' he mocked ruefully. 'That handsome Greek devil certainly knows how to pick them.'

Jemma stiffened instantly. 'Are you trying to be insulting?' she demanded.

His eyebrows shot up in surprise. 'Of course not!' he denied. 'It was actually supposed to be a compliment.'

'Your technique needs polishing, then,' she informed him, and turned away, searching the milling throng for a glimpse of Leon.

The man's soft laughter shivered down her naked back. Then suddenly he appeared in front of her and stuck out his hand. 'Jack Bridgeman,' he introduced himself.

Jemma glanced down at the hand then back into his amazing eyes. 'I know who you are,' she said drily. 'One would have to be blind and deaf not to—wouldn't one?'

The eyebrows shot up again. 'Now who's being insulting?' he challenged.

She sighed, accepting that he was right, and took the proffered hand. 'Jemma Davis,' she said. 'Most definitely not a name you will recognise!' She sent him a rueful glance.

He grinned. 'Let's go and find you a drink,' he offered, and took her arm.

She let him guide her away, out of one room and into another—just as crowded—but where a superbly stocked bar stood against one wall, manned by white-coated waiters.

She saw Leon then, standing in a group of laughing people, his arm draped across the shoulders of the woman in the white dress. Red-hot humiliation swam up from the pit of her stomach to encompass her whole being. He had forgotten all about her! In among this lot she was nothing, and she felt like a nothing.

I hate him! she thought and took a deep gulp at the contents in the glass that had arrived in her hand. The cocktail almost took her head off, whatever was in it burning like fire down the back of her throat. It took all her control not to fall into a fit of choking. Beside her, Jack Bridgeman watched her lazily.

'Whose is this party, anyway?' she asked him when she felt able to speak.

'Hers,' he informed her, nodding his head towards the woman who was draped all over Leon.

'Oh,' said Jemma, looking down to hide the jealous look in her eyes. Why had he bothered bringing her if he preferred his hostess's company?

'She looks like a fluffy black kitten when in actual fact she's a dangerous, money-eating panther,' he added with a small smile which didn't meet his eyes. 'Which is why you only see her with men who stink of the stuff—like your Mr Stephanades.'

'He is not *my* Mr Stephanades,' Jemma denied, and realised bleakly that that was probably the truest thing she'd allowed herself to say about her relationship with Leon since it began.

'Good,' Jack Bridgeman said. 'So let's you and me go and dance.'

He took her arm again, but Jemma hesitated, her eyes helplessly drawn to the other side of the room where Leon still stood talking with their hostess. Should she just boldly go over there and claim his attention? The urge to do just that was burning alongside the jealousy in her blood. But, even as the idea entered her head, she watched Leon draw the woman closer and lower his dark head to drop a kiss on her upturned cheek.

She looked away, her eyes glazed over with hurt. Then, on a mammoth gathering-together of all her pride, she smiled brightly at Jack Bridgeman. 'Dance, you said?' She took a final gulp at her drink and put down the glass. 'Just lead the way and I'll follow!'

He guided her on to the tiny dance-floor. 'Right,' he said as he drew her into his arms. 'Tell me about yourself, Jemma Davis!'

So she did, prattling on about anything so long as it kept her mind off Leon. By the time they had circled the room for two records, she was beginning to relax and enjoy herself, Jack's easy manner and needle-sharp sense of humour actually managing to make her laugh.

'Ah,' he sighed ages later when the music went even slower and he took it as a cue to pull her closer and slide his fingers lightly along her uncovered spine. 'You've no idea how much I've been aching to do this. You're the first woman, Jemma Davis, whose back view has managed to turn me on even before I took a good look at the front!'

'Charming!' she mocked. 'Was that supposed to be another one of your compliments?'

He grinned boyishly. 'Oh, don't worry, sweetheart,' he murmured huskily. 'The back view is a delightful appetiser but the front is positively lethal!'

'You aren't so bad on the eye yourself,' she told him, flirting deliberately. 'Despite the sex symbol image,' she tagged on teasingly.

'Or because of it, maybe?' he suggested drily.

Jemma studied his face for a moment, then shook her head. 'No,' she decided. 'Sex symbols tend to strut their wares for all to see. You don't strut, so I'll give you the benefit of the doubt and presume your ego is not as big as it's reputed to be.'

'You precocious little madam!' he choked, not slow on picking up on her hidden meaning. 'Give me five minutes alone with you and I may well just prove you wrong there!'

He stopped dancing, teasing her by grabbing hold of her wrist and turning towards the doorway. Still laughing, Jemma tugged against his grip—then saw Leon leaning against the open door a mere two feet away, his black eyes fixed on her, and she went still beside the other man.

'Ah,' said Jack, seeing the reason for her stillness. 'Do I see a royal summons written in those frightening eyes, ma'am?' he mocked.

'Yes, I think you do,' Jemma confirmed with a nervous little laugh.

Jack looked down at her, his expression suddenly serious. 'You don't have to go with him, you know,' he said quietly. 'All you have to do is turn your back on him and that will be the end of that. Stephanades is not a man who likes to make scenes. He won't come after you.'

Jemma knew that, even as she stood there, locked in silent battle with those eyes; she knew that Leon was not going to make a single move towards her. That pride-shrivelling gesture was down to her.

'So?' Jack prompted, bringing her eyes flickering up to meet his sardonic ones. 'What are you going to do?'

'Goodnight, Jack,' she said a trifle ruefully. 'And— thanks.'

Reaching up, she kissed his lean cheek, her eyes full of a silent apology before she turned and walked slowly to Leon. 'I'm ready to leave if you are,' she told him stiffly.

He didn't answer or even acknowledge her for the space of ten turbulent seconds, his gaze fixed on something beyond her shoulder—which had to be Jack, she assumed, or Leon's eyes would not look so shiveringly steely. Then his dark lashes flickered, forming two perfect, sleepy arches over his eyes as he lowered them to her hot, defiant face.

'More than ready, *agape mou*,' he answered quietly, and to her utter confusion he smiled. Not a threatening smile nor even a deriding smile, but a warm, if slightly rueful smile, and his hand, when it reached out to curve around her waist, was surprisingly gentle. He drew her against him and kissed her softly on the lips. As he drew away again, his gaze slid over her shoulder and hardened fractionally. But when it returned to her it was warm again, revealing no hint of anger at all. 'Let's go,' he said.

She went willingly enough. But her confusion at his manner did not leave her, so nor did her own stiff manner. Whatever he was up to, she decided as he saw her indulgently into the car then came around to join her, she wasn't going to let down her guard to find out. If he was trying to soften her up before jumping on her for kissing Jack Bridgeman, then he was in for a disappointment! she decided huffily as they drove away. And she answered his light conversational remarks with monosyllables, her own mood becoming blacker the lighter his become.

'You are angry with me,' he decided after several attempts to draw her out failed.

'What could you have done to make me angry?' she drawled.

'All but dumping you as soon as we arrived there is a good enough reason,' he admitted. 'Business, I'm afraid,' he shrugged.

Funny business, Jemma derided bitchily on an upsurge of that evil jealousy she was beginning to feel so familiar with.

'At least you fond some light relief with Jack Bridgeman. You enjoyed your—dance?'

This is it, Jemma thought with a slight stiffening of her spine in readiness. 'I enjoyed his company very much!' she stated coolly. 'He was charming and attentive and a very good dancer, and without him I would have been bored to death!'

'Then I must thank him next time I bump into him,' was all Leon said to her outright provocation. And changed the subject.

To her surprise and confusion, he didn't refer to it again. And over the ensuing weeks she noticed that, wherever they went and whoever tried to make a pass at her, he never revealed any hint that it concerned him overmuch. He often left her alone while he went off to 'discuss business', as he called it, and, no matter whom he found her with when he eventually came looking for her, he was always aggravatingly at ease about it.

It was meeting Tom on the stairs a couple of days later that put the missing piece into the puzzle, when he asked if her boyfriend had got over his fit of jealousy. And it clicked suddenly that Leon had not liked revealing that hint of weakness in himself when he'd reacted jealously to her kissing Tom. Since then he had gone out of his way to show the opposite reaction, as if he was determined to quash any idea she might develop that he thought more of her than their relationship suggested.

Which was—what? she asked herself. Lovers. Nothing more, nothing less. Jealousy grew out of deeper feelings. Feelings that Leon just did not have for her. Or if he had, for one brief blinding moment when he'd seen her kissing Tom, he had firmly squashed them. And if he could do that so easily, then they couldn't have been very strong feelings.

The week after the party, he went off to New York for a week. She had come to realise that his business commitments seemed to flow equally between London and New York—with a trip to his head office in Athens thrown in only very occasionally. Friction with his father, she suspected—not that Leon had ever spoken about it. But his expression was tight-lipped whenever she broached the subject of his family and, remembering what Cassie had once said about a family rift, she drew her own conclusions.

While he was in New York, she missed her period. Jemma was not overly worried about it since her cycle had never been that reliable at the best of times, and she accepted that the physical and emotional stress she had taken on since Leon had probably helped to throw her out of sync.

For the next few weeks he remained in London. And they were barely out of each other's company. Josh had found out about them by then, and his disgust was un-veiled. 'Are you crazy?' he cried. 'Of all the bloody men in London you have to fall for Leon Stephanades! I just don't bloody well believe it!'

'He's what I want,' she answered simply. 'And for as long as he wants me I'm happy.'

'And when he doesn't?' he challenged brutally.

Jemma shrugged to mask the ache his words evoked. 'I'll cross that bridge when I come to it,' she said.

Josh sighed heavily, but let the matter drop.

Late Friday afternoon, when she was just considering packing up to leave for the weekend, the telephone rang. Leon sounded grim and irritable. 'Something has come up,' he said. 'I'm afraid this weekend is out.'

'Oh.' Her disappointment sounded clear in her voice. 'So when will I see you?'

'God knows,' he sighed. 'I have to be in New York on Monday and will be away the whole week. I'll call you,' he said, and rang off.

She went out with Trina and Frew on Saturday night, meeting up with all her old friends for the evening. But she felt restless and out of place among them. Leon occupied her whole mind these days and she couldn't seem to enjoy anything that did not include him.

On Monday, she woke up feeling dreadfully ill. 'Tummy bug,' she said to Trina, and took herself back to bed. By Wednesday she was beginning to feel a bit better, but only marginally. Still, it was enough to send her back to work.

Josh took one look at her and remarked, 'You look shocking.'

'Thanks,' she drawled. 'That does make me feel better.'

'Beginning to get to you, is it?' he drawled out cynically. 'Hanging on to a man like Stephanades wears a woman down, doesn't it? And I should know,' he added bitterly. 'I've had his leftovers, after all.'

Jemma winced at his cruelty, hating the ugly twist he had put on Leon's friendship with Cassie. And it made her realise that if there had ever been a seed of love growing inside him for the other woman, then it was well and truly dead now.

Leon noticed her poor state of health the moment he saw her. When she explained, he just continued frowning and said, 'Are you sure it isn't something worse than just a stomach virus? You look pale and you've lost weight.'

She just shrugged the question away. 'You know what it's like with these things. Once they get a hold of you they can take an age to go away again. I'm feeling a whole lot better, really.' So long as she didn't eat anything, she added grimly to herself.

He ran his eyes over her slender figure. 'Perhaps you need a break,' he murmured thoughtfully. 'When did you last have a holiday?'

'Christmas,' she told him, smiling wistfully. 'I spent it in Barbados with Trina. We had a great time.'

'Lots of men, I suppose,' Leon growled, pretending to sound jealous, but Jemma now knew better. Leon did not get jealous—and why? Because he did not care enough for her, that was why. Not with any emotions which really mattered, anyway. He fancied her like hell still, could still lose himself in her body with enough passion actually to shock her sometimes. But as for any deeper feelings, they just did not exist.

He was in London for a week. And they saw each other every night. But her continuing virus and all the late nights began to take their toll on her, and she was actually relieved when he went away again.

She only wished she could have a break from Josh, too. He had become a boor to work for, his bitterness with Cassie reflecting in his attitude to all women—including her now. He was brusque and impatient all the time. 'If you can't do your work to your usual standard, Jemma,' he snapped at her one day when she had somehow mislaid a file he wanted, 'then perhaps you should start thinking about either giving up Stephanades or giving up this job!'

'This thing with Cassie has really soured him,' she confided in Leon when Josh had been worse than nasty all day and she felt exhausted by the time she met Leon for dinner that night.

'What do you expect?' he countered coolly. 'To be tricked as Cassie tricked him is, in my opinion, the ultimate betrayal.'

Something in the way he said that hit her on the raw. It was if he was warning her—try that kind of trick on me and see what you get!

She shuddered and changed the subject. But that weekend her manner towards him cooled slightly. It wasn't that she wanted it to, it was just that, after over two months of living exclusively for him, she was beginning to realise how hopeless the relationship really was. After all, there was still the nice Greek girl with the dowry waiting somewhere for Leon to give in to family pressure and marry. And she could suddenly appreciate what Cassie had meant when she'd said, 'What chance does a not-so-nice English girl with nothing to offer him but a great body have against all of that?' None, Jemma acknowledged, and began to wonder if it was perhaps time to start weaning herself off Leon Stephanades.

If he noticed her coolness, he said nothing, not until Sunday evening, that was, when he was dropping her off at her flat, and he surprised her by saying, 'Before you go, Jemma, I have a proposition I want to put to you.'

'A proposition?' she repeated curiously.

He nodded, his expression unusually grim. 'Next week, I close a take-over deal I have spent the last year putting together in New York,' he informed her. 'When it is done, I will be hard put to come up for air during the following few months while I drag the company up to the standard the Leonadis Corporation requires of all its subsidiaries. The company is in a bad way, has been badly run, badly managed, and recklessly bled by its owners to the extent that nothing short of some ruthless tactics will give it a hope of surviving the next few months...' He paused, watching her face. 'I will not be able to come to London as often as I have been doing,' he explained. 'Maybe not at all, the way things are stacking up.'

'So...' Jemma kept her voice steady by sheer strength of will '...this explanation is your way of saying goodbye?' she assumed, feeling the weight of knowledge bearing heavily down on her. She had been so busy trying to cool her own feelings for him that she had not noticed that Leon was going through a similar process for her!

But his reaction surprised her. 'No!' he denied, reaching out to haul her across the gap separating them so that he could issue a hard, angry kiss to her lips. 'What in hell gave you that idea?' He actually sounded shocked enough to bring weak tears floating into her eyes. 'Damn you, Jemma!' he muttered. 'I have never known such a difficult woman to read as you! You spend the whole weekend giving me the cold shoulder—then have the cheek to suggest it is me who is doing the cooling off!'

'I haven't been feeling well...' she offered as a very lame excuse for her behaviour.

He nodded curtly and kissed her again. 'And you think I have not noticed—or, worse, have not cared? I said I had a proposition for you, and it is with your poor state of health and my refusal to let you go out of my life that I offer it! Come with me,' he invited huskily. 'Next weekend will be the last I can promise to devote to you here in London. But if you will come with me to New York, I will promise to devote every moment of my spare time to you!'

'M-me—to New York?' she choked, hardly daring to believe he was offering it. 'But—my flat—m-my job!' She sat up and away from him, trying to make her whirling brain think.

'You said yourself that Tanner is becoming impossible,' he inserted. 'Losing that job will not come as any hardship—except financially, of course,' he added when she sent him a wry glance. 'But I am not just asking you to come to New York, Jemma,' he went on softly.

'I am asking you to move in with me, be my woman. Allow me to worry about all the practicalities of your life while you just worry about making yourself beautiful for me.' His hand slid beneath her hair to curve her nape. 'I want you—need you there with me, *agape mou*,' he murmured softly. 'Will you come?'

Well, will you? she asked herself for the hundredth time that same night. She lay alone in her small single bed, missing him, missing the warmth of his body curled up against hers, missing the scent of him, the soft sound of his breathing when he slept.

Will you—can you give up everything here for the man you love, knowing that he wants you to only because his desire for your body has not yet worn out?

Not that Leon saw any of that as a reasonable excuse not to give him an answer straight away. 'What is there to think about?' he'd demanded when she'd asked for time to do just that. 'Either you want to be with me or you do not. It really is as simple as that!'

'Is it?' she'd mocked, then sighed heavily. 'You're asking me to uproot my whole life for you, Leon!' she'd cried. 'I would have to be crazy not to think carefully before making that kind of decision!'

'Or not crazy enough about me to know instinctively that where I am is where you want to be!' he'd suggested, his pride touched.

'And for how long would I be welcome there?' she'd thrown back. 'I am to uproot while you simply exchange one of your many addresses for another. What happens to me when you grow tired of me and find someone to take my place?'

'That can work both ways, you know,' he'd countered. 'I am not so conceited that I don't see the way you can enjoy other men's company!'

'Nor am I so conceited that I don't see how you enjoy other women!' she had snapped.

'I am not promiscuous!' he'd stated haughtily.

'And neither am I!'

He had sighed. 'No, I know you are not,' he'd agreed, then sighed again, heavily this time. 'Look,' he'd said, 'I am not ready to lose you, my darling! Do you think I would be making a proposition like this one if I were?'

She'd thought about that, and had to decide that no, Leon was nothing if not scrupulously fair. He would not be asking her to change her whole life for him if he did not think the change worth her making it.

It had been her turn to sigh, to soften her manner. 'You're right,' she'd conceded. 'And I apologise for implying that you would. But you must see, Leon,' she'd gone on quickly before the triumph grew too bright in his black eyes, 'that I have to have time to think about this!'

A point he had conceded grudgingly. 'Next week,' had been his parting shot. 'I will be here next week and I will expect your answer then.' The kiss he had issued then had been so sweetly possessive that she had almost caved in and said yes there and then. But something held her back, she wasn't sure what.

Just as something held her back from telling Trina, she acknowledged with a frown, wondering if it was the same elusive 'thing'.

Sighing, she turned over and punched her pillow into a more comfortable shape. She didn't know what she was doing, lying here in the middle of the night wondering about what she was going to do when she already knew, if she was honest, how she was going to say, Yes, please, to him, because, from the first time she'd ever seen him, she had not been able to deny him anything.

Then, two things happened in quick succession during that week to change her mind irrevocably.

The first was on Wednesday morning, when Josh came striding into the office with all of his old energy back. Instead of stalking straight by her desk with a grunted 'hello' as had become his habit, he stopped in front of her, leaned down and banged the desk-top in exhilaration.

'She got rid of it!' he announced in gleaming triumph.

'Got rid of what?' she frowned. 'Who?'

'Cassie!' he cried. 'She got rid of it, and I suddenly feel so free it's like walking on air!'

She didn't know where it came from, but, on an acid surge of bitter, vile-tasting disgust, she shot to her feet, a dark red tide of anger swimming across her vision as she struck out with the flat of her hand.

'You bastard!' she breathed out contemptuously as he leapt back in stunned amazement. 'You nasty—selfish—evil bastard! How dare you come in here dancing with joy when you should be huddling in some dark corner somewhere cringing in shame? God, you make me feel sick!'

And she was, violently sick, only just making it to the bathroom before she threw up. When she went back to her office, Josh wasn't there, the door to his office firmly shut. She didn't even think twice about it. She just gathered her personal things together and walked out. She could not go on working for a man who could behave like that. It went against the grain of every moral code she believed in.

Trina was in the flat when she got in, working on her books at the kitchen table.

'I'm ill,' was all Jemma could manage to say. 'I'm going to bed...' She turned away, her senses still too sickened by Josh to want to talk even to Trina about it.

But Trina had other ideas. 'For God's sake, Jemma!' she snapped out impatiently. 'Don't you think it's about time you faced it? If you leave it much longer, the shock of it could do you some physical harm!'

'What shock?' she asked blankly. 'Face up to what, for goodness' sake?'

Trina stared at her, her expression almost comically tragic. 'Come on, sweetheart,' she sighed. 'You're not that thick! He'll notice if you're not careful, and then where will you be?'

Notice? she repeated in her head. Notice what?

But even as she was thinking it, she was beginning to tremble, her body lowering itself carefully into a chair, eyes going dark with horror.

'Oh, God!' she choked, and buried her face in her hands.

Pregnant. The elusive little thing which had held her back from giving Leon an answer to his proposal. The same elusive little thing which had held her back from telling Trina what he had offered. And the same elusive thing that had made her react so violently to what Josh had said.

Pregnant. Her body had known for weeks, her mind probably for just as long! Only she'd blocked it out, refusing to so much as think about it—not daring to think about it because she knew exactly what it would mean to her relationship with Leon.

'Oh, God!' she whispered again and slipped into deep, silent tears.

'Oh, Jemma!' Trina sighed, coming to squat down beside her. Then, exasperatedly, as if she couldn't help herself, 'What did you think was happening to you when you've gone two months without a period?'

'One,' Jemma choked.

'Two,' insisted Trina, then very gently, 'Darling, you haven't had a period since you started going out with Leon! Think about it—that's been over two months now!'

Two—two months? She stared unbelievingly into Trina's anxious eyes, then burst into tears again. She was right—so damned right! And she'd just thrust the knowledge away as if doing so would make the situation go away! But it hadn't—well, it couldn't!

Oh, what was she going to do?

*   *   *

'When will you tell him?' Trina asked quietly later when the storm of shocked weeping had abated and she'd managed to get Jemma undressed and into bed.

'I'm not going to,' Jemma said thickly. 'How can I, Tri?' she demanded at Trina's expression. 'After going through all of this with Josh and Cassie, he'll think I've done it to him deliberately!'

'But this is nothing like the situation which developed between those two fools!'

'Isn't it?' It looked exactly the same to Jemma.

'I just knew he was too much for you to have your first love-affair with—and I was proved right, wasn't I?' Trina said angrily. 'I mean, look at you!' she sighed, glaring down at the pathetic picture Jemma presented huddled beneath a mound of blankets with her face all swollen and pale. 'Heartbroken and pregnant. It couldn't be worse!'

'Call a spade a spade, why don't you?' Jemma muttered, then felt the rise of fresh tears again. 'I love him, Tri!' she whispered. 'I just couldn't do it to him!'

'All right—all right!' On another sigh, Trina sat down on the edge of the bed and stroked a soothing hand over Jemma's tumbled hair. 'So,' she murmured. 'What will you do?'

'I don't know yet.' Jemma made an effort to control herself, pulling herself up into a sitting position and wrapping her arms around her bent knees. 'I just can't think yet—how could I have been so stupid as to ignore what was happening to me?' she choked out contemptuously, lowering her head so that the curtain of hair tumbled about her face.

'Maybe it isn't what we think,' Trina suggested. 'Maybe I've jumped to the wrong conclusions about what's wrong with you.'

Jemma's face came up again, blue eyes stark with tears and mockery. 'Do you honestly believe that?' she drawled.

'No.' Trina shrugged, so did Jemma, and a silence fell around them for the space of a few dull minutes.

'How the heck did it happen, anyway?' Trina demanded suddenly. 'I thought you were being careful.'

'We were!' Jemma declared. 'But that first time, I— we——' She stopped and blushed, then went on huskily, 'After that he used something——'

'Do you mean to tell me that that—highly experienced rake took you without protection that first time?' Trina jumped in in disgust.

Several times, Jemma corrected silently, unable to keep the soft smile from her lips when she remembered that first earth-shaking night in his arms. They'd both been too lost in each other to give protection a single thought!

'But that alters everything, Jem!' Trina said eagerly. 'It means that he is as much to blame as you are! And even Leon himself can't deny that!'

Jemma stiffened, her vulnerable face closing up suddenly. 'I will not trap him into a situation he has no wish to be trapped into,' she said firmly.

'Marriage, you mean? It's what you deserve.'

'Any kind of situation!' Jemma declared. 'Marriage and babies are not what Leon wants from me,' she added dully.

'Yet he *has* invited you to go and live with him in New York!' Trina persisted. 'That has to mean he cares something for you, doesn't it?'

'Nothing alters the fact that I will not trap him with this baby,' she stated stubbornly. And was glad she had the rest of the week to come to terms with what she must do instead.

CHAPTER SIX

JOSH rang the next morning, asking stiffly if she was returning to work or not. Trina spoke to him. Jemma couldn't. And he took her resignation without argument, promising to send her what he owed her in the way of salary by post. Jemma suspected that after what she'd said and done yesterday he was probably as relieved to see her go as she was to leave.

Leon rang each evening as he always did. And Jemma used these calls to begin distancing herself from him. He noticed. He had to do. She was cool and polite and rather vague if he touched on anything too intimate—and cried herself to sleep every night.

By Thursday his voice was terse and aggressive. 'I will be arriving back about five tomorrow night,' he informed her. 'Shall I expect you at your usual time, or not?' His sarcasm cut, even though she knew it was well deserved.

'Of course,' she said, biting down on her bottom lip to keep the ever-ready tears out of her voice. 'I'll be there about six.'

She spent Friday reinforcing her resolve to finish this with as much style as she could manage. Luckily the dreaded sickness seemed to be leaving her alone today, so she felt and looked a lot better—physically, that was. Inside was a different matter. Inside she felt as if she was splitting slowly into two.

She took nothing with her to the house, simply because she was not intending staying long.

Leon opened the door to her knock. He looked deeply into her sombre eyes and his own expression closed up tightly as he stepped to one side to let her go by him.

He barely gave her a chance to remove her coat before he got ruthlessly to the point. 'I presume by your manner all week that you have decided to remain here in London.'

She paused in sliding the cream raincoat from her shoulders, a pang so painful that it held her breathless for a moment, slicing right through her. He looked so wonderful to her hungry senses, so big and dark and achingly withdrawn. He had showered recently, and his hair lay in a sleek, damp gloss flat against his well shaped head. And gone were the business clothes he would have travelled home in and instead he was wearing a casual pale blue cotton shirt and grey trousers that hung loosely over his flat stomach from the fashionable pleating at the waist. His eyes were so dark that she couldn't see anything in them but a grim reflection of her paler self, his mouth a thin straight line that told her that, like herself, he had prepared himself for this meeting.

Despair suddenly drenched her, and she remained standing there, wanting to run to him, wrap her arms around him, soothe that closed expression from his face, make him smile, laugh, pick her up and hug her tightly while he gave her that first long satisfying kiss they usually shared at this moment.

But, 'Yes,' she answered him huskily, and followed him with her eyes as he simply grimaced and walked into the book-lined room to pour them both a stiff drink.

She shook her head in refusal when he offered her a glass, unable to hold his gaze when he remained standing in front of her, sipping out of his own glass while he studied her pale face narrowly.

'Have you found someone else?'

'No!' Her head shot up, sheer surprise at the question making her answer honestly, but later she realised it might have been easier on both of them if she'd had the foresight to lie and use another man as her excuse. As it was, things only got worse.

'Leon—you knew last week that I wasn't very—enthusiastic about the idea of leaving everything I know and feel safe with, to go to New York with you!' she reminded him with an appeal in her voice. 'And the more I've thought about it, the more sure I've become that it just isn't the right thing for me to do!'

'Why not?' Nothing else, just the blunt enquiry.

Jemma swallowed on her dry and tense throat. He was not going to make this easy. 'There's no future there for me,' she said dully.

He took his time absorbing that reply, his eyes so black they were impossible to read. Then his mouth tightened again and he said coolly, 'If you're angling for a marriage proposal, Jemma, then you're in for a disappointment. It is an institution I have no intention of joining, whoever I have to sacrifice to keep that vow.'

That brought the sparkle back into her eyes. She glared at him angrily. 'And I never for one moment so much as considered marriage as an option!' she snapped with an honesty he would never be able to appreciate. 'But neither am I prepared to become any man's mistress! At the moment we share a relationship,' she went on more calmly, 'in which I have a job and a home of my own and a level of independence which allows me to keep my pride and self-respect. But the word "mistress" is an ugly one, Leon. Yet that is exactly what I would become if I agreed to come and live with you in New York.'

Silence met that, and it came down around Jemma like a death-knell, sinking her into a helpless despair because she knew, as she watched Leon turn slowly and go over to pour himself another drink, that she had achieved exactly what she had set out to achieve.

The end to their relationship.

'So, this is it.' It was he who put it into words.

'Yes,' she answered huskily. 'You said no commitment, Leon,' she reminded him, seeming to need to hammer the point home for her own benefit as much as his. 'Honesty and loyalty, you said. Well...' She took in a deep breath, her voice beginning to tremble along with her body. Inside she was weeping just as she had wept every night this awful week. 'You've h-had my loyalty, and now I am giving you my honesty.' Liar, a small voice jeered inside her head. You're lying to him with every word you say! She flinched but ignored it. 'I c-care for you deeply, but...'

'Not enough to trust yourself to me,' he finished for her.

She shook her head, the tears managing to find a crack in her defences and creep into her eyes. He saw them and sighed, slamming down his glass to come striding over to her. 'No,' he muttered as he took her into his arms. 'Forget I said that. It was unfair and unworthy. In fact, when I have had time to come to terms with your decision——' he was deliberately instilling a lighter tone into his voice '—no doubt I shall even learn to admire you for it. But,' he sighed, lowering his head so that he could kiss the trail of salty tears away, 'at the moment I see only the end to a very special period in my life, and for that I hurt too, just as these tears tell me you are hurting.'

He hurts, she repeated achingly to herself, and wanted to hold him tightly to her until his hurt went away. Her arms went around his waist, revelling in the feel of warm, taut skin beneath her fingertips, her face burrowing into his throat on this one last surrender to this weakness she had which was him.

'Ah, Jemma,' he murmured heavily. 'Are you sure I cannot change your mind?'

She shook her head, but held him all the closer, and he laughed softly. 'But maybe it would be enjoyable if I were at least to try?' he suggested.

He lifted her chin, his eyes dark and intent as they ran over her pale, unhappy face, then he sighed again, and his mouth came down to meet with hers. His hunger and her need met in a powerful kiss which verged on desperation.

Their tongues tangled, their bodies melting together as though they were drawn like that by some power beyond their understanding. It wasn't sexual, it was something else far more disturbing. With the prospect of a final parting and the emotion which came with such an end, it was as if each fine nerve-end was pushing its way up to the surface of her skin in an effort to absorb every last ounce of him into her.

A muffled sob broke in her, and Leon groaned, his mouth hot as it buried itself in her throat. 'Change your mind,' he murmured huskily. 'Neither of us is ready to give this up.'

Jemma came spiralling down from whatever heights she had been flung to, with a shiver that racked her whole frame. 'No.' She shook her head, having to force her fingers to break the anguished grip they had on him.

His own hands slid up her body to curve her ribcage then tightened painfully, stopping her from moving away from him. 'Then give us this weekend!' he urged. 'One last wild, beautiful weekend, Jemma, to lose ourselves in each other before we must part!'

Oh, she was tempted, so severely tempted. She wanted him and he wanted her. It was like manna from heaven to her aching heart. But she dared not give in to it. She knew even as she hovered on that fine dangerous line between self-delusion and sanity that just in this last week since she accepted her condition the changes in her body had been too obvious to dare take the risk of him noticing them—and ultimately drawing the right conclusions.

So, 'No,' she breathed, and took the last vital step which would separate them forever. 'I'm sorry, Leon, but I can't.'

'Cannot or will not?' he mocked, changing from sweet to bitter in response to her rejection.

'Can't, Leon—can't!' she choked out wretchedly, then whirled away from him, the tears blinding her eyes as she snatched up her coat, desperate to get away from him before her control snapped altogether.

'Jemma——!' She was at the door when his harsh voice brought her to a stumbling halt. She didn't turn, and there was a tension in the short silence which followed that sent violent shudders of reaction spurring through her body while she prayed that he would just let her go while she still had the strength to do it. 'Take care of yourself,' was all he said in the end, quietly and so gently that she almost crumpled in a heap of misery on the floor.

She nodded her downbent head. 'And you,' she whispered, then left quickly without looking back.

He didn't try to stop her again, and for that she was grateful. Her heart was breaking and if she'd stayed in his company a moment longer he would have seen it happen.

Jemma was sitting at the kitchen table, flicking through the morning newspaper while chewing desultorily on a slice of lightly toasted wholemeal bread when the doorbell rang.

'I'll get it!' Trina called from the hallway, and Jemma grimaced with relief, glad to be doing what most pregnant women did first thing in the morning and keeping as still as possible while she coaxed her stomach not to give up on the meagre amount of food and liquid she had managed to swallow.

Only most women lost this inconvenient malady three months into their condition. Jemma, on the other hand, was now well into her fifth month with no let-up in the sickness. Morning sickness, afternoon sickness, evening sickness—you name it, she suffered it.

It showed, too, she grimly acknowledged as she felt that old familiar churning begin in her stomach. For an otherwise perfectly healthy pregnant woman, she looked hagged to death. The inability to hold down more than half of her daily intake of food had certainly taken its toll.

She weighed less now than she had at the beginning of her pregnancy. And, although her hair shone with a thick golden lustre that her doctor assured her was the clearest sign that she was doing fine, the rest of her looked thin and gaunt—except for the bulge forming in front of her, that was. She glanced at it. Her mound, she called it. 'The lump'. 'Leon's parting gift', since he had never quite managed to come up with anything for that one special gift he owed her.

But as for the rest of her—she wouldn't give it mirror-space if she could avoid it: bruised eyes, pale cheeks. And a distinct lack of energy which seemed to require every ounce of determination to get her through each day.

It really wasn't fair.

A bad dose of the flu just after she'd broken off with Leon hadn't helped. If she'd thought the virus she hadn't had had been bad enough, then the real thing had proved to be twice as awful. Trina blamed it on all the emotional stress she had been under. And Jemma could not really argue with her about that. It had seemed, that day she'd challenged misery to do its worst and told Leon that she was not prepared to uproot her whole life for him, that the emotional stress could not get any worse. She had been wrong. The constant sickness kept her in a permanent state of taut readiness for the next bout. Fear for the baby's health had her creeping about like an invalid, afraid that at any moment she would dislodge the poor thing with her constant retching. And if the doctor had not assured her that despite it all—the flu and the sickness—the baby was doing fine, she had a suspicion she might well have given up the ghost and taken to her bed to die languidly.

She felt so rough. And she missed Leon. It hurt most of the time even to think about him. Yet she thought about him constantly, a never-ending circle of self-inflicted misery which in no way helped her present condition.

On a brighter note, Leon's take-over of the huge American shipping company had made the headlines several times this week, the papers singing the praises of the Greek tycoon who had managed to turn the company's fortunes around with such devastating speed. This morning's article said:

> Leon Stephanades, the strong arm of the Leonadis Corporation, has worked a miracle on the old company. With heavy investment and a bomb up the backsides of all those who believed themselves to be on to a cushy number under the old regime, he has managed to secure contracts that have set all those mocking doubters in his own family by their ears. His father took time off from his second son's wedding celebrations to concede last night, 'Leon has a nose for a good risk', as their stock on the market hit an all-time high. What Dimitri Stephanades forbore to add was that this success came despite the way he had tied his son's hands over the last year by refusing to give him *carte blanche* on this venture. One must ask, though, if it is sensible to tie the hands of a man like Leon Stephanades. And whether maybe it is time the old man abdicated his power to his elder son.

Jemma had read and re-read the article, simply because it told her more about Leon than she had ever learned from the man himself. Namely the fact that there was someone above him who could tie his hands. Then there was the fact that he had a brother at all.

'Well, lump,' she murmured to her slowly steadying stomach, 'your daddy is certainly a clever devil. No wonder I was worth dropping if this was what he was going after.' And she stared down at the two aerial photographs where the vast square acreage of part of New York's dockland was shown in 'before' and 'after' comparison. One photo showed its dry docks half deserted of both products and people, but in the other the whole place seemed to be a veritable hive of constructive activity.

'Jemma . . .' Trina's voice sounded tentative to say the least.

'What?' she asked, glancing up from the newspaper article.

'Trouble,' Trina bluntly announced and put an envelope down in front of her.

Jemma stared at it, a cold shiver of alarm skittering down her spine. Like Trina, she recognised the bold scrawl instantly. And, like Trina, she knew it could only mean trouble. 'Hell,' she muttered.

Trina pulled out the chair beside her and sat down. 'What can he want?'

'I don't know.' In all honesty, she had not expected to hear from Leon again. This had come as a shock.

'Hadn't you better open it and find out?'

I would much rather not, Jemma thought ruefully, but even as she was thinking it her fingers were working tremulously at the seal. Dry-mouthed, she stared at the few hastily scrawled lines before their meaning began to sink in. It said:

I am due in London Friday. I would like to see you. Have dinner with me? Shall call for you at eight. L.

Her heart gave a pathetic little leap, then began to palpitate so fast that she could barely breathe, her lips going as dry as her mouth. The mere idea of him being so close as in London made her want to weep with longing. Then she was instantly hardening herself. There was no room in her life for that kind of weakness now.

'What does it say?' Trina asked.

'Nothing,' she said, and handed the note to Trina.

Trina read it slowly, her usually open face studiedly impassive, then she looked at Jemma. 'I think you should go,' she elected quietly.

'Is that your idea of a joke?' Jemma derided, sitting back in her chair and pointedly placing her hands on the top of her rounded stomach.

'No.' Trina shook her head. 'I mean it. I think you should go and meet him . . . I think it's time, Jemma, for you to ask for his help.'

'Don't be stupid!' she snapped, going to get up from the table, but Trina stopped her by grabbing hold of one of her hands.

'You'll stay here and hear me out!' she insisted. 'Jem,' she appealed at the other girl's glowering hostility, 'carrying his baby has been harder than you anticipated! It's weakened your health! Left you without a job——'

'I quit working as a temp because I couldn't stand being shunted around all over the place!' she reminded Trina angrily. 'It had nothing to do with my condition!'

'It had everything to do with your condition!' Trina sighed. 'You were off sick so often they had to let you go—you know they did!'

'Which has nothing to do with my meeting Leon!'

'It does when you're only just managing to exist on social handouts,' Trina said bluntly.

'Thanks,' she muttered, thinking of all the things she had to go without so that she could pay her share for living here. 'Rub it in, why don't you?'

'I am not trying to rub anything in!' Trina cried. 'Jem—Leon has a responsibility to help you!'

'He does not!' she snapped, and walked away.

'When are you going to stop being so stubborn?' Trina demanded, following her with a determined look on her face. 'What right have you to decide what Leon may or may not want? It's no use you tripping off to the bathroom in the hopes I won't follow you because I will!' she warned as Jemma turned in that direction. 'You're on your last legs, love, and if Leon is holding out a hand towards you you've got to take it!'

She turned at that, blue eyes flashing in a way they had not done for months now. 'Since when has he become flavour of the month for you?' she gibed. 'I always got the impression that you thought him the worst thing to happen to me!'

'I did,' Trina conceded. 'And I still do. But it doesn't alter the fact that he did happen, and the results of that are staring me right in the face!'

'Hear that, lump?' Jemma said acidly to her stomach. 'Your aunty Trina is having a go at you!'

Despite herself, Trina had to laugh. 'I wish you would stop talking to that thing as if it were alive,' she protested drily.

'It is alive,' Jemma pointed out. 'And my problem.' Her hand possessively covered the lump. 'No one else's.'

'Wrong,' Trina disagreed. 'That lump has a father. Do you honestly have the right to deprive it of that?'

No answer—simply because Jemma did not have one, since it was one of the very things she had agonised over herself since she and Leon had split up.

'I'm still not going to meet him,' she said with a stubborn thrust of her full bottom lip. 'Leave it, Tri!' she cried when Trina opened her mouth to argue again. 'Just—leave it!' she whispered, and turned away, leaving Trina standing there staring helplessly after her as she locked herself in her bedroom.

By the time she reappeared, Trina had left the flat to go to work. In the spotlessly clean kitchen, lying like a pointed threat in the dead centre of the scrubbed table, was Leon's note. Jemma sat down, drawing the piece of paper towards her.

She read it slowly, wanting to read more warmth into the few short sentences than was actually there and knowing that it would be folly to try. Friends, she reminded herself. We parted friends—or at least we didn't part enemies, she corrected ruefully, remembering the way she had run out of the house. 'Take care of yourself,' he had said, as a friend would say to a friend. This note was just a friend wanting to look up a friend while he was in town.

He would be hurt when she turned him down. 'It hurts me to turn you down,' she whispered, a flush of hot tears blurring her eyes. But she folded the letter back into its envelope anyway. 'I'm sorry, lump,' she murmured as she stood up again. 'But it just can't be.'

When Trina returned late that afternoon, Jemma was tossing a light salad in the kitchen. 'I'm whacked,' the other girl said, throwing herself down into a chair. 'We've had to spring-clean a six-bedroomed town house from top to bottom today. You know what these old houses are like,' she sighed. 'All twelve-foot-high ceilings with intricate cornices specifically designed to gather dust.' She stretched tiredly then rotated her shoulders, wincing when the aching muscles protested. 'Tomorrow we re-hang the curtains—huge heavy things with swags and flounces—but at least when we've done that it'll be finished.' She picked up her mug and gulped thirstily at her tea.

'That's the house near Grosvenor Square, isn't it?' Jemma asked lightly. Since giving up her own job, Jemma had taken over Trina's office work for her and over the last month or two she had become quite familiar with Maids in Waiting's customer roll.

Trina had gone still, her face coming out of her mug to look narrowly at Jemma. She wasn't a fool; she knew exactly what Jemma was going to do. With a jerk,

Jemma fished a letter from her pocket and placed it on the table. 'Tomorrow is Friday, and I want to be sure Leon will receive this or I would have sent it by post today,' she explained. 'Will you take it for me, Trina—please?'

Trina was a long time answering, her expression difficult to interpret as she looked from Jemma's pale, defensive face to the sealed envelope then back again. Feeling uncomfortable, Jemma shrugged her shoulders awkwardly. 'I would take it myself,' she murmured awkwardly. 'Only I have a hospital appointment tomorrow and...' She shrugged again; Trina knew how long and tiring those expeditions were.

'All right.' Trina picked up the letter. 'I'll take it,' she agreed, but the look of grim disappointment on her face made Jemma feel worse.

Was she becoming a heavy weight around Trina's neck? she wondered suddenly, and felt a new fear rip right through her. Without Trina, she just didn't know what she would do!

Trina went out with Frew that night. When they came back, Frew was unusually quiet, his responses terse when Jemma attempted to speak to him. She took herself off to bed in the end, presuming they'd had some kind of a row and deciding to leave them to it.

The next day Trina had left for work before Jemma had surfaced, and was still out when she trudged back home from the hospital late that afternoon. Trina had left a message on the answersphone, warning Jemma that she was going out with Frew directly from work and not to expect her back again tonight. It wasn't unusual. It was Friday, and Trina often stayed over at Frew's flat on the weekend—much the same as she had done with Leon, she recalled bleakly.

It was warm outside, and unusually humid for September, with a distinct threat of a storm in the air. She wasn't hungry, but she made herself a jug of freshly squeezed though heavily diluted orange juice and drank thirstily at a glass of it before taking herself off for a long soak in the tub in the vague hope it might ease some of the tension out of her body. The hospital was pleased with her progress, but not with the continuing sickness that dogged her still. They had booked her in for another scan next week—just to check a few things out: nothing to worry about, they had assured her.

But she was worried. Anything out of the ordinary where her baby was concerned was a worry. All right, so her weight was still too low, but they were all pleasantly surprised by the size of the baby! And, despite the sickness, she made sure she ate good nourishing food. So, what else could go wrong?

Sighing, she pulled out the plug to let the bath-water escape, then levered herself into a standing position and turned on the shower, allowing the clean cool water to wash over her for long minutes before loading her palm with shampoo and washing her hair.

Six-thirty, she noted as she walked into her bedroom wrapped in a fluffy white towel. She had managed to waste a whole hour and a half in the bath without thinking of Leon once! All she had to do now was think of something which would fill her mind for the rest of the long empty evening.

She would go out! she decided impulsively. Take in a movie. Jack Bridgeman's latest was playing at the local. It was supposed to be good. And really, anything was better than sitting here mooning over a man who was even further beyond her scope than a great big movie star.

Hastily, she pulled on fresh underwear then hunted out a pair of white stretch leggings and a navy blue baggy T-shirt that adequately covered her lump. Clipping her hair into a tortoiseshell slide at her nape, she applied a bit of blue eyeshadow to her eyes and a pink gloss to her lips, then snatched up her bag. If she hurried, she would just make the first film, she decided, opening the flat door.

Then she froze.

CHAPTER SEVEN

'GOING somewhere?' a deep, soft, beautifully accented voice questioned. 'How fortunate I managed to catch you, then.'

Jemma couldn't move. One hand had a white-knuckled grip on the door while the other had stalled in the process of throwing the strap of her bag over her shoulder. She was shocked—horrified. Yet, despite it all, her wide, staring eyes drank him up, her senses stinging into bright startling life as they recognised their master. He was wearing white, a white summer shirt and white cotton trousers, the complete lack of colour in the outfit only helping to enhance the rich dark brown of his skin. He looked big and lean, essentially sexual and innately dangerous.

Dangerous. She picked up the word and tasted it warily. Dangerous he certainly was. Pulsing with danger, throbbing with it, standing there smiling at her while his eyes burned with it.

She blinked and swallowed, trying to pull herself together. 'W-what are you doing here?' she heard herself asking foolishly. 'D-didn't you get my note?'

'Note? Yes, I got your—note,' he confirmed, then, while she still stood there staring at him, she watched as the danger metamorphosed itself into blinding anger. 'Inside,' he snapped, taking hold of her wrist to twist her fingers off the door so that he could push her back into the flat in front of him.

The door slammed shut. Jemma stood there trembling while he maintained his grip on her wrist, then he was pulling her into the sitting-room, before spinning her to face him and grasping her by the shoulders. 'Were you ever going to tell me?' he demanded harshly.

She sucked in a short, fast, shaky breath then let it out again, her heartbeat beginning to race out of control. 'I d-don't know what you're talking about,' she stammered constrictedly.

'No?' It was so quietly spoken, so silkily produced that he made her shiver in real fear of him for the first time. He moved, lifting his hands from her shoulders to spread them over her swollen stomach. She gasped at the blatant intimacy of the action, and his eyes burned darker. 'Then to whom does this belong?' he demanded.

'I...' She tried to move away but he stopped her simply by snaking one hand around her back and sandwiching her between the two. 'M-mine,' she whispered threadily. 'This baby is mine.'

'No father?' he mocked. 'An immaculate conception, maybe?'

She flushed at his sarcasm, but stubbornly clamped her lips together and lowered her eyes from the burning threat in his. But he waited. Oh, how he waited, drawing out the silence between them until she thought she could actually hear their child's heartbeat throbbing beneath his resting hand. Perhaps he thought the same thing, because his hand moved, stroking in a light caressing gesture as if to soothe the agitated child. And in answer the baby kicked and with a sharp intake of breath Leon went still.

'You feel that?' he enquired huskily. She nodded, swallowing. 'He speaks to his papa, *agape mou*. Are we to waste any more time on your lies, or are you going to be honest with me for once?'

'Honesty!' she flashed, her chin coming up aggressively. 'You want honesty, Leon?' Angrily she pushed his hands away. 'Well, I honestly don't want you touching me!'

'I was not touching you, I was touching our child!'

'My child—mine!' she flashed. 'This child is my mistake. My responsibility. I didn't ask you to come here. And I don't know why you have! But if it is to tell me how wrong it is for me to have this baby, then you're too late!' The blue eyes were spitting challenge, the fierce, threatening challenge of a woman protecting her unborn child. 'They won't abort this baby without a damned good medical excuse!'

'Abortion?' he choked, his black brows drawing downwards over his eyes. 'What the hell are you talking about? I never mentioned the word!'

'No,' she agreed, feeling the monster nausea begin to claw at her insides. 'Because I never gave you the chance! I'm not Cassie,' she stated thickly. 'And no man is going to dance with joy at the loss of *my* child!'

'Cassie?' he said bewilderedly. 'What does she have to do with any of this?'

'N-nothing,' Jemma stammered, running a shaky hand through her hair. In all honesty she was so staggered at him turning up like this that she barely knew what she was saying. 'Sh-she let Josh off the hook in the most unequivocal way she could, that's all,' she told him bitterly. 'But I didn't put you on the hook, Leon!' she cried. 'So you have no right to come here throwing your weight about, telling me what I should——'

'Cassie aborted her baby?' Leon interrupted in a voice that said this was news to him.

'Yes,' she whispered, feeling decidedly shaky on her legs all of a sudden.

'And you think,' he persisted slowly, as if he was having trouble taking it in, 'that I would have expected you to do the same?'

No! Oh, God—no! she thought, and shuddered in horror at her own vile words. How could she accuse him of something like that? She knew—*knew* he was not that kind of man!

'I'm sorry,' she apologised huskily. 'Of course I never thought that of you.'

His chest moved harshly. 'Well, that is something, I suppose,' he muttered, yet still flaying her with a contemptuous look.

'I'm sorry,' she whispered again, feeling so guilty that she wanted to cringe.

'Oh—sit down!' he ground out, and it was only when he took hold of her arm and helped her into a nearby chair that she realised how badly she was trembling.

'Good God,' he muttered, 'you barely look fit enough to support yourself, never mind the child you carry! How the hell have you let yourself get into this state?'

'I've been ill,' she mumbled distractedly.

'Sick with your own deceit, I should imagine,' he muttered unsympathetically.

'Who—who told you about the baby?' She asked the question which had been burning at her brain since he had arrived, distinctly unsurprised by her pregnant state.

He was glaring at the floor, and for a moment Jemma thought he wasn't going to answer her, then he glanced up and grimaced. 'Your flatmate, who else?' he said, and watched what colour she had left leave her face at this ultimate betrayal.

'She was supposed to just deliver my note,' she whispered painfully.

'Which is exactly what she did do,' Leon nodded. 'Only fate happened to take a hand in things. I arrived home—early, since I had managed to catch an earlier flight—to find her at my door. What happened next is between myself and your friend,' he stated grimly. 'Except to add that she is more of a friend than you deserve. We will, of course, invite her to our wedding.'

That thoroughly shook her, bringing her head up sharply to stare at him. 'But I can't marry you, Leon!' she cried.

'And why not?' he demanded haughtily. 'You have other crimes to lay at my feet, maybe? Other sins I am to be found guilty of without trial?'

She flushed. 'No, of course not. But——'

'Then perhaps it is a sin of your own which makes you stare in horror at the idea of marrying me?' he suggested. 'Maybe there is more to this than even your best friend divulged to me? Something, perhaps, to do with the man you were on your way to meet tonight when I—surprised you with my arrival?'

Man—what man? She frowned, having no idea what he was talking about.

'The man your note spoke of,' he illuminated for her. 'The man you informed me you are heavily involved with.'

Oh. Jemma flushed and lowered her eyes as enlightenment dawned. She had forgotten all about the lie she had made up for not wanting to see him.

'Maybe,' he went on grimly, 'this man is the father of your child, hmm? Who is he?' he demanded. 'Anyone I know? Is he a better lover then I? Is that why you dropped me for him? Regarding your condition, I must also presume that you met him long before we parted!' He eyed her narrowly. 'Could it be that your flatmate and I have jumped to too many conclusions all round?'

'Stop it!' she choked, unable to bear any more. 'You know I'm not like that! When did I ever give you the impression that I could be?'

'Devious, you mean?' he asked. 'A liar and a cheat?'

She went white at his words, the sickness beginning to crawl up inside her. 'I w-want you to leave,' she whispered, coming shakily to her feet.

'You don't like these accusations?' he asked. 'They offend you as deeply as your accusations offended me?'

So that was it. He was simply getting his own back on her in the most insulting way he could think of. 'I s-said I was sorry,' she murmured. 'What else do you want me to say?'

'You can tell me whose child it is you are carrying.'

'Yours!' she choked out wretchedly. 'You know it's yours!' Then she turned and made a dash for the door.

At least he saved her the ultimate humiliation of watching her while she was wretchedly sick, caught off balance by the urgency with which she had thrust him out of her way so that she could run to the bathroom. By the time he had joined her there, she was already hanging weakly over the bowl, and after a moment's stillness he turned and walked away.

She was sitting limply on the edge of the bath when he returned. He said nothing, but there was a grimness about him as he reached behind her for the bath sponge then ran it under the wash-basin tap before squatting down to apply it to her hot, clammy face and neck.

'You've lost weight,' he observed. 'How the hell does a woman in your condition lose weight?'

She shook her head, unable to utter anything at the moment while she fought this never-ending battle with herself. It didn't help that he was so close, the warmth of his body and the familiar subtle scent of his after-shave making her head whirl all over again.

'Why did you do it, Jemma?' he gruffed out suddenly. 'What did I ever do to make you mistrust me so?'

'I didn't mistrust you,' she sighed. 'I just—mistrusted our relationship.'

He lifted her chin with his hand, his black eyes boring into her weary ones. 'Yet I offered you more than I have ever offered any woman. Did this count for nothing?'

'How arrogant,' she scoffed. 'You offered to make me your kept woman and went out of your way to make your opinions on marriage clear! Just as you were very clear about your opinions on women who set out to trap men by getting pregnant!' Impatiently she knocked his hand away, then picked up a towel to dry her face. 'You didn't leave me much choice, did you?' she muttered finally.

He didn't answer, but his expression revealed enough for her to know she had managed to make him think.

'Tell me why you look so pale and thin,' he demanded on a complete turn-about of subject.

Jemma grimaced to herself. What cannot be defended, must be ignored! she noted drily. 'I've been ill, I told you,' she said, 'with the flu.' She lifted an unsteady hand to her hollowed cheek. 'It—dragged on a bit, but I'm beginning to recover now.'

He ran his eyes over her. 'And the child?' he asked. 'Has he suffered through this—flu?'

She found her first smile for that, a rueful one that Leon could not begin to understand. 'No,' she said. 'He hasn't suffered.'

Something passed over his face, a look gone before she had a chance to interpret it, but it had a disturbingly relieved quality about it. He threw down the sponge and straightened, then seemed uncertain as to what he should do next.

'Are you all right now?' He ended up referring to her for advice. 'Should you lie down for a while or something...?'

'I'm fine now,' she assured him flatly. 'Thank you.'

He frowned. 'Then why are you still sitting there,' he wanted to know, 'as if you have decided to take root?'

Jemma glanced impatiently at him. 'Because my legs are not quite ready to support me yet, that's why!'

'Then why didn't you say?' Instantly he was gathering her up in his arms and walking out of the bathroom. 'Where?' he enquired, stopping in the hallway.

'The kitchen,' she said, feeling the bitterness of helplessness bite at her nerves. 'I need a cool drink.'

He nodded, moving smoothly through the kitchen door to deposit her carefully on a chair. 'Stay there, I'll get it.' He went to the fridge, bending to peer inside then coming out with the jug of orange. 'Will this do?' He looked at her questioningly.

She nodded and he busied himself then, finding a glass. He put it down in front of her then poured out the orange.

'It looks disgustingly weak to me,' he said, eyeing the mixture dubiously.

'It's how I like it.' She didn't add it was the only way she could take it.

'Do you mind if I refrain from joining you and make myself a coffee instead?' he requested.

'Help yourself,' she invited, adding drily, 'So long as you don't place it under my nose, that is.'

'Your stomach is that sensitive?' He had moved over to the kettle and was checking the level of water inside.

'Only when I laugh,' she joked, feeling at least some of the tension ease out of her overwrought muscles.

He turned and grinned at her. 'That bad, eh?'

'It depends on your definition of bad.' She grimaced. 'Trina thinks it horrifying. Watching me has put her off having children for life, I think!'

'Ah, Trina,' he murmured, loading his mug with two heaped teaspoonfuls of instant, no less. 'A very good friend you have there, Jemma. One of the best, I would say.'

Jemma sat back in her chair, eyeing him narrowly. 'Quite a mutual-admiration society you two have set up together, isn't it?' she drawled, recalling the way Trina had spent every available moment the day before singing Leon's praises. 'I remember a time when you could do nothing but bite each other's head off!'

'We share a mutual interest,' he defended mildly. 'That kind of thing can draw the most unlikely people together.'

'Enough to make one betray another friend?' she suggested succinctly.

'Betrayal?' He glanced thoughtfully at her, then returned his attention to pouring hot water on his coffee.

'Trina did not betray you.' He did not even try to mis-understand. 'If anything, she betrayed herself in her ef-forts to maintain her loyalty as your closest friend.' Bringing his drink with him to the table, he sat down then looked levelly at her. 'Did you know she has turned down an offer of marriage from her accountant because she is so concerned about what will happen to you if she did marry him?'

The easier mood shattered, sprinkling around her like a million and one shards of sharp, piercing glass.

Leon watched her for a few minutes, sipping calmly at his coffee while the full impact of what he had just said sunk indelibly in. Then he set down his cup and said smoothly, 'Now we talk weddings, Jemma.' And her eyelashes flickered as she focused on his grimly de-termined face. 'Ours, not your friend's. She has taken enough interference from us.'

The 'us' was a mere sop. But it stated its point well enough. Trina must have been feeling as if she was being pulled in two, what with her sick, pregnant and alone friend tugging her heartstrings on one side, and the man who wanted to marry her tugging frustratedly on the other!

It was no wonder she'd gone to Leon. She must have seen him as her only salvation!

She swallowed, seeing herself as Trina must see her, and felt the rise of nausea bite into her stomach again. A weight. She had become that weight around her best friend's neck.

Slowly, she lifted her eyes to Leon's. 'What do you want me to do?' she asked, and Leon nodded once firmly, as if her reply moved her up a couple of notches in his estimation.

'I want you to pack your things and be ready to move out of here by tomorrow lunchtime,' he said, giving his instructions in much the same way he would give them to anyone under his power—with a level but an unchallengeable tone. 'By the time I come to collect you, you will have left a long letter for your friend, convincing her not only that she did the right thing in confiding in me, but that you also can't thank her enough for it. You will tell her how ecstatic you are. How much in love!' He slid the words out mockingly. 'Then you will thank her nicely for being the good friend she has been to you, and wish her good luck and goodbye. But at no point will you so much as hint that you know anything of her own frustrated wedding plans,' he warned. 'Because she is no fool, that one, and she will guess that I have used my knowledge of it to coerce you, which will in turn only make her feel wretched and guilty—which we do not want, do we, Jemma?'

She shook her head, too full up with aching tears to speak.

'Good,' he said, and got up. 'Now we go out and eat,' he announced as if the rest just hadn't happened.

'I can't,' she whispered thickly, the idea of food appalling her delicate stomach.

'You can.' His hand, firm on her arm, lifted her out of the chair. 'And you will.' He looked determinedly into her defeated blue eyes. 'If I have to carry you there with a bucket stuck beneath your nose, you will come—and eat. Understand?'

Understand? she echoed dully. She understood everything. She had just become one of Leon's possessions, to do and be whatever he demanded of her.

Surprisingly, the nausea subsided again. It hovered for a little while longer, threatening to send her running, but after a couple of deep controlling breaths of the warm humid air it left her, and she climbed into his silver Mercedes feeling more settled inside than she had for days.

Weeks—months? a little voice inside her head quizzed. Now there was a loaded concept, she mocked it. But not one she wished to dwell on right now.

He had her back at the flat by ten-thirty. 'I won't come in,' he informed her as the car engine died. 'Get some sleep,' he instructed, lifting a hand to comb a stray lock of hair lightly from her cheek. 'And try not to dwell too deeply on your lot, *agape mou*. I am not such a bad catch, surely?'

She glanced at him, her blue eyes clashing with his in the darkness of the car. 'The point is,' she posed, 'would the catch be caught if it weren't for a heavily baited hook?'

'You are referring to my lot?'

'I just don't understand why you're doing this,' she explained, then sighed heavily. 'I never asked for marriage from you, Leon, and still don't expect it from you!'

'You would prefer I set you up in a nice little semi-detached house somewhere in London suburbia?' he suggested. 'With a nice little allowance with which to live on while you rear my child?'

'I would rather you just leave me alone to get on with my life in my own way!' she snapped, retaliating to his disparaging tone.

'Your life?' he snapped out angrily. 'What has your life got to do with this? Or my life come to that?' He turned on her, his hand once again making the possessive statement by coming to lie over her stomach. 'This is the only life that counts now, Jemma!' His eyes flashed in the late summer darkness, naked with a stunning sincerity. 'What you or I want for ourselves from now on can take only second place to this! And this needs both a mother and a father! Which is exactly what he will get, if I have to drag you screaming to the altar by the roots of your beautiful hair!'

He moved jerkily, throwing himself away from her and back into his seat to sit glaring out of the car window as though the world beyond it had suddenly become his enemy while the space inside the car hung with the echo of his passionate vow.

And it had been a vow, she acknowledged as she sat there and shook in reaction. A vow which put all her high-minded principles about leaving Leon his freedom while she struggled to bring their child up alone to shame.

As if he could read her thoughts, Leon twisted his dark head to look at her, his voice calm now but grim when he spoke. 'We will not speak of this again,' he decreed. 'The deed is done, our futures set.' He paused, levelling one final implacable look at her, then leaned across her to open her door. 'I shall be back here by noon tomorrow. Be ready.'

The next day, she was packed and waiting when his knock sounded at the flat door. He stepped inside, his gaze running briefly over the loose pale blue cotton sundress she was wearing without revealing his thoughts.

She wondered what he was seeing when he looked at her like that—the desirable woman he had once taken in his arms so passionately? Or did he see the pale shadow of that woman she felt she had become?

'Ready?' he asked, glancing at the neatly stacked suitcases standing against the wall.

She nodded mutely.

'Nothing else?' He seemed surprised, and Jemma forced her dilatory tongue to move.

'I've left a few boxes of things in my room. Nothing important,' she told him. 'They can be picked up—whenever.' Her accompanying shrug said she didn't care.

'Then they come now,' he said decisively. 'You won't be coming back here again, Jemma.'

She shivered, the words having a much more final ring to them than just thinking them all night long had.

CHAPTER EIGHT

'No,' JEMMA refused outright, staring in horror at the room he was in the process of placing her suitcases in. 'I won't sleep with you, Leon!'

Turning, she stalked back down the stairs and into the sitting-room, where she stood staring angrily out of the window. How dared he? If it wasn't bad enough him taking her straight from her flat to a private clinic where he proceeded calmly to stand right beside her while a top London gynaecologist put her through just about every embarrassing examination a woman could be subjected to, he was now just as calmly expecting her to share his bed!

'I hate you!' she whispered without turning when she heard him come into the room. 'How could you be so bloody insensitive?'

'Are we about to discuss our sleeping arrangements or the fact that I insisted on being present throughout your examination?' By contrast he sounded smooth and beautifully cool!

'Both!' she snapped. 'I find both intrusions on my privacy utterly distasteful!'

'It is not the fact that I intrude on your privacy that you find so distasteful, Jemma,' he argued drily. 'It is the fact that I intrude at all!'

She went to deny it, then snapped her lips tight shut over the words. She did see him as an intruder, so much so that she was still trembling from the indignity of it all. She felt trapped, wrung out and trampled on. In less than twenty-four hours, Leon had completely taken over her right even to think for herself! And she was just beginning to understand what it was like to become a Leon Stephanades business take-over. The iron hand in the velvet glove! she called it helplessly, because he was doing it all with the kind of quiet authority she found impossible to fight against.

'You could at least have shown some—taste and allowed me to lose my dignity in private!' she threw tensely at him.

'And what about my rights as a prospective father to be interested and concerned for you and the child?' he countered. 'You think it did not move me as deeply as it moved you to see the actual evidence of our child moving—living inside your womb? Yes...' he taunted softly when his words surprised her enough to turn and stare at him. 'I saw your expression when the scanner showed our perfectly formed child, *agape mou*. I saw the glow of pride and the more obvious feelings of relief when the good doctor assured us that everything is well. You think I did not experience the same emotions, should not be allowed to experience the same things?'

'That isn't what I meant!'

'Isn't it?' He walked towards her, his expression grim suddenly as he made his usual statement by placing both hands on her swollen body. 'We are a unit,' he declared. 'Three parts of one whole, joined by the irrefutable existence of our child—ours!' he repeated with soft ferocity. 'And the quicker you come to terms with that, the more comfortable we can all become with it!'

Comfortable? He honestly believed she would learn to be comfortable being with a man who could turn his back on the woman, yet was prepared to put up with her because she was suddenly the mother of his unborn child? 'Which does not include my having to sleep with you!' she declared stubbornly.

'It does if we are to have any hope of making a success of this marriage,' he said grimly.

'We are not married yet!'

'But we will be in two days' time!' Another shock announcement that set her poor head reeling. 'And wherever you decide to sleep tonight, Jemma,' he warned, 'you will sleep with me from then on!'

He meant it. The hard flash of his eyes said he meant it, the possessive grip of his hands said he meant it, and the dark, angry sense of frustration she felt burning inside told her she just did not have a single say in it. But she had one last try. 'Can't you at least give me a little time to get used to the idea of us being together like this before I have to——?'

He was already shaking his head, grim-faced and immovable. Jemma sighed, feeling the threat of tears block her throat. 'Then I repeat,' she whispered thickly, 'you are an insensitive brute!'

'Perhaps,' he conceded, coming down from anger to a rueful kind of self-mockery when he sensed her defeat. His hand moved from her body to her shoulders, then slid gently to her throat, his long fingers burrowing into her thick, shining hair to cup her nape and his thumbs gently pressing beneath her chin to bring her face up to meet the smile softening his eyes. Her heart flipped over, her senses beginning to buzz as the look awakened all those weaknesses she had always harboured for him. 'Surely, *agape mou*,' he murmured, 'it is not so long ago that we slept together that you could have forgotten how good it was for both of us?'

'I don't remember sleeping much!' she snapped, trying to fight both him and her own wayward feelings.

Leon laughed softly. 'But this time will be different,' he promised, adding ruefully, 'If only because the good doctor prescribed rest and no excitement!' Taking her by surprise, he kissed the top of her nose, then released her. 'Now,' he said on a complete change of subject, 'I want to know your opinion of boats.'

'Boats?' She just stared blankly at him. 'What have boats got to do with anything?' she demanded bewilderedly.

'A lot if you like them,' he replied. 'Nothing if you are prone to seasickness. Your body has enough to contend with from that particular malady without my wanting to worsen it.'

Jemma lowered her eyes, refusing to tell him that she had not felt sick once since he arrived back in her life. The doctor had hinted at worry and stress as being the culprit. And she was beginning to believe he was right.

Heart sickness, not morning sickness? that small voice inside her head suggested.

'Are you?'

'What?' She glanced up at him, having lost the thread of the conversation in the tangle of her own troublesome thoughts.

'Prone to seasickness.' He sighed out patiently as if he were talking to a child.

'No,' she answered. 'I used to belong to a sailing club when I was a teenager. And I did a bit of sailing with Trina last Christmas when we were in Barbados without feeling any ill effects. But I don't see——'

'Good,' he cut in. 'Because I have one—or,' he then amended wryly, 'I have a yacht. The doctor prescribed rest, good food and no excitement for the next few weeks while we bring you back into decent health, and I cannot think of a better place to ensure all three than cruising the Greek islands on my yacht with the most exquisite chef your tastebuds have ever encountered. What do you think?'

What did she think? For the first time since he had walked back into her life, she felt the stirring of pleasure. 'I think it sounds lovely, but...'

'No buts,' he dismissed arrogantly. 'We will pick the yacht up in Corfu on Tuesday, and work our way south through the Ionian islands—a good idea for a honeymoon, eh?'

Honeymoon? Jemma couldn't help it, she shuddered, the whole idea sounding utterly hypocritical to her. 'You don't have to put the rest of your life on hold for me, Leon,' she told him huskily. 'I am quite aware that I must have messed up your...schedule enough as it is!'

'Have you?' he murmured thoughtfully. Then, 'Yes, I suppose you have,' he agreed. 'Still,' he added with a careless shrug, 'that is what we will do. Now,' he went on before she had a chance to make up her mind whether to be hurt or not by his answer, 'I'm hungry. Let's go and see what there is to eat.'

They ate in the kitchen with no formality, just as they used to do before. And Jemma was rather surprised at how easily they slipped back into their old easy ways. By the time they had cleared away, her long day had thoroughly caught up with her, and she couldn't stifle a weary yawn.

'Bed,' Leon commanded, turning her towards the stairs. 'There are five bedrooms up there, *agape mou*. Take your pick.' It was a reassurance and the allowance of one small victory for her. Jemma accepted it with a tired smile and a contrary sense of disappointment inside. 'Take what you need for the night, but leave your cases where they are until the morning. I have several hours of work to get through before I can retire,' he added. 'So I will say goodnight now.' He bent to press a light kiss against her lips.

She responded—couldn't stop herself even as she damned her own weakness for it. As Leon drew away, it was her lips that clung, her soft sigh which whispered between them filled with helpless longing. Opening her heavy eyes, she then wished she hadn't when she found herself staring into his, so dark with knowledge that it made her want to weep at her own pathetic vulnerability.

'I wish I could really hate you,' she whispered helplessly.

'Do you?' He smiled strangely, as though the idea that she could hate him was not that impossible to imagine. 'Well,' he murmured, his gaze roaming over her pale, wan face, 'I will be giving you no reason to hate me tonight, so go to your bed. And be at peace.'

And she was, totally, utterly at peace, Jemma decided two weeks later as she lay in the depths of a sublime laziness on the sun-drenched deck of Leon's disgustingly luxurious yacht, shading the sun from her eyes with one hand while the other held up a letter she had just received, via the speed launch that came skimming across the water from the mainland to pull alongside them every morning, bringing Leon any business papers that might need his attention.

It had surprised her that he had not shown the least inclination to get back to the cut-throat excitement of a powerful tycoon's life. But, if there was one new thing she had learned about him during these weeks—and there had been several—then his ability to play the sloth had been the most surprising. Oh, he worked, certainly. A man with his responsibilities could not simply close shop and forget about it completely. But he restricted his time spent shut up in his fully equipped stateroom to a few hours every morning and the same in the afternoon while she took her enforced rest. Between times, he became a lazy, good-natured, intoxicatedly charming companion, willing to indulge her in anything from lying next to her here on the sun-deck for hours on end without bothering to move, or taking her out in the on-board speedboat to the nearest island where she could enjoy her newly acquired skills at snorkelling around the rocks.

The improvement in her health had been remarkable, even to Jemma herself. The sickness had gone, she had acquired a very carefully nurtured but rather attractive golden tan to her skin, and a bloom to her features which was a one hundred per cent improvement on the hollow-eyed pregnant wraith she had been threatening to become.

She had stopped being self-conscious of her new maternal shape within hours of arriving on the yacht, forced to dismiss how she looked by the sheer heat of the sun and the utter arrogance with which Leon had walked up to her while she stood on the sun-deck in one of her long, baggy T-shirts, boiling hot and wondering if she dared slip away to the delicious coolness of her cabin—which was more like a luxury hotel suite with its *en-suite* bathroom and delicious air-conditioning—so that she could hide away from yet another day of fierce Greek sunshine. But Leon had had other ideas. He had simply reached out and coolly stripped the T-shirt right off over her head! Then, while she'd stood there red-faced and struck dumb with mortification because she was left wearing only the briefest pair of cotton panties, he'd taken his time exploring every inch of her and even gone as far as to grip her wrists and wrench them apart when she had attempted to cover herself.

'Now we have got that embarrassing little moment out of the way,' he had drawled eventually, 'perhaps we can begin to relax and enjoy this cruise as it was meant to be enjoyed?'

Since then she had lived in one of the bikinis Leon had provided for her—sometimes topless, sometimes not—or in a light cotton shirt when it was sensible to cover herself from the sun for a while.

They lived, ate and slept on the yacht, and her feet had only touched dry land on the few rare occasions Leon had let them visit a secluded bay for the odd picnic. And in general she was more than at peace with herself, she was happy. At least, she amended ruefully, she was happy within the confines of the contented little bubble she was living in just now.

Which was probably why she was looking at Trina's letter without reading a single word of it. She was afraid her friend might say something that could burst the bubble. Remind her, perhaps, of the realities she had so successfully thrust aside.

'Read,' she told herself firmly, and forced her eyes to focus on the tightly crushed and very rushed lines of words. Trina began:

> Guess what! I'm married! And if you think yours was a disgustingly rushed affair, well, wait till you hear about mine!

Jemma grinned, settling herself back to enjoy a good read. Frew, it seemed, had taken Trina off to Barbados and married her on a beach! They had been away a week, and been back in London a week. Trina was now madly trying to find a house for them.

> Frew's flat is just too small for us both, what with all my office stuff littering up the place and the work he brings home piled everywhere. We should have thought more about it before deciding to live at his place. It may be nearer to his office than our flat was, but at least ours had your bedroom free to turn into an office. Still, it's too late now. I closed the lease on our old place, so now we've just got to find something bigger.

The flat was gone. Jemma felt the tiniest bit of disturbance within her bubble—as if some of the air was trying to escape. No home, she realised. Nothing in London to go back to if she ever felt she needed to. It felt a bit strange, realising just how totally she was now dependent on Leon.

The sound of approaching footsteps almost had her falling off her lounger in an effort to snatch her straw sunhat up off the deck and quickly stuff it on her head.

Leon appeared, just as she had settled herself back on her lounger looking as though she hadn't moved in hours.

He came to stand beside her, silently offering her a tall glass of iced water and two small pills. Making heavy weather of it, she pulled herself into a sitting position, exchanged the glass and pills with him for the letter, then found herself studying him covertly from beneath the shadowed brim of her hat.

He was wearing nothing more than a faded old pair of dark grey shorts—his usual attire when aboard the yacht—and he looked big and lean and brown, the dark cluster of crisp black hair on his broad chest curling downwards over the flat planes of his stomach to disappear beneath the elasticated waist of his shorts.

Her senses leapt and she looked quickly down and away. It never had done her any good to feed her weak love of simply looking at him, she noted drily. Her senses always ended up spoiling it.

And her senses were not allowed to ignite, she drily reminded herself. Because this was a 'no sex' marriage. Ironic really, when before it had been a 'no marriage' sexual relationship! He had kissed her only once since the day they married when he'd turned her into his arms and placed his cool lips against her own in what she could only describe as a civil seal to their civil marriage!

Since then—well, the matter of sharing a bed had never arisen again. And, other than the fact that she sunbathed in next to nothing, for most of the time they were both scrupulously respectful of the other's privacy.

Quite a change from those long lazy weekends they'd used to spend invading each other's privacy as if it were their right!

Still, she mused, it had its benefits. Without the added ingredient of sex to complicate their relationship, she and Leon had actually become quite good friends. And although she sometimes awoke in the middle of the night, her body tight and hot with a need which could some-times hold her tense in desperation, she had never so much as considered giving in to the feelings and creeping into the room next door and Leon's bed. Mainly, she acknowledged ruefully, because Leon had not shown any inclination that he still wanted her physically. He flirted and teased in that light-hearted way friends did with each other, but she had never glimpsed, even once, any hint that he could still desire her as a lover.

Not that she blamed him. With a small grimace, she glanced down her reclining body where their child thumped rhythmically against the tightly drawn walls of its home. She had to be about as undesirable as she could get!

'This is from Trina?' he asked, breaking into her thoughts to wave the letter at her.

'Oh, yes,' she confirmed. 'You can read it if you want,' she invited, popping the pills into her mouth and swal-lowing them down with the water. She did it all without really thinking about it now. It had become a ritual she had grown used to over the weeks. If it wasn't Leon fol-lowing her around making sure she took her daily dose of iron, it was one of his stewards.

'You do not mind?'

Jemma just shrugged. 'There's nothing in it I wouldn't want you to read. Just Trina going on about weddings and flats that are too small...' She fell into con-templative silence, unaware that Leon studied her clouded face for a few moments before hitching his hips on to the nearby table and bending his dark head to read.

'Your friend sounds happy, *agape mou*,' Leon mut-tered quietly after reading the letter.

'Mmm,' Jemma replied absently, sitting up to hug her arms around her bent knees.

'So, what has she said to—upset you?'

'Upset?' she echoed. 'I'm not upset,' she denied. 'Just...' A sigh broke from her and she went silent.

Leon frowned, his dark eyes fixed thoughtfully on her. 'You wished you had attended her wedding?' he persisted despite her denial.

Jemma shook her head. 'It wasn't that kind of wedding, was it?' A romantic beach wedding in the Caribbean was not the kind you invited all your friends to!

Leon glanced at the hurriedly written sheet of paper in his hand, his puzzled frown darkening his face as he quickly scanned the chatty but pretty innocuous sentences searching for a clue to what had put that gloomy expression on her face.

'She closed the lease on our flat,' Jemma murmured suddenly. 'I spent four of the happiest years of my life there. It was my home, and I know it sounds silly, but it's suddenly hit me that I no longer have one. No home. No place in England I can actually call my own.'

'But we have a home in London,' Leon pointed out. 'I don't see the problem.'

'Your home.' She glanced at him over the top of her knees. 'Yes, I know. But it isn't——' The same, she had been going to say, but could see from his expression that he didn't understand. Couldn't understand what it felt like to be made suddenly aware that you had nothing—nothing you could call your absolute own, even if it was only a silly little flat on the cheap side of London with draughty windows and a bath-tap that leaked. She didn't even have a best friend any more. Trina belonged to Frew now, just, she supposed heavily, as she belonged to Leon.

Glancing thoughtfully at him, she wondered if he would understand if she tried to explain, then decided it was at least worth a try. 'I spent most of my younger years moving from house to house, town to town with two parents who were constantly unfaithful to each other. One would find him or herself a lover and go off for a month or two then they would come back and the other would be off.' She shrugged, knowing that really did not explain anything more than that she had two faithless parents. 'I never knew from one week to the next which one of them I would be living with. And I never got a chance to develop long-term friendships with any children of my own age because I was constantly being shunted around. Fresh starts, they called it,' she mocked. 'Which meant different towns, different schools, different parents—different homes.' She shrugged again, her blue eyes bleak. 'When they died and I moved to London to work I answered an advert in the paper for a flatmate, which was how I met Trina. She, and that little flat, gave me the first taste of real stability I had ever known. Four years,' she murmured softly. 'Belonging to someone and somewhere. And now it's gone again.'

'And you do not believe that I can give you all of that and for much longer?'

'I don't know, do I?' she shrugged, twisting to put her feet to the sun-heated deck. 'We married because of our baby, not because it was what either of us particularly wanted to do—not the best of foundations to build a stable relationship on. Still,' she concluded as she came to her feet, 'that was not the point I was actually trying to make. I was trying to explain to you why the flat and Trina had been so important to me, and why therefore I was suddenly feeling their loss.'

She went to turn away, but Leon stopped her by catching her hand. 'They have not been taken from you, Jemma,' he said quietly. 'They have just been replaced, that's all.'

With what? she wondered, and gained no comfort at all from his words. 'It's time for my rest,' she said, and sent him a small hollow smile before slipping her hand out of his and walking away.

When she awoke again, it was to the sound of the yacht's engines throbbing steadily beneath her.

She got up, dressed quickly in a simple pair of white calf-length baggy trousers made of a lightweight cotton, and a pale blue cotton over-shirt, then went in search of Leon, eager to find out where they were going.

She found him sitting at the table beneath the shaded awning on the sun-deck, reading business papers over a tall pot of Greek coffee. Like her, he had changed into lightweight trousers and had pulled a short-sleeved white shirt on to cover his darkly tanned chest.

He looked up and smiled as she approached, getting up to pull out a chair for her and seeing her seated.

'Where are we going?' she asked curiously.

'One moment and I will answer,' he said, striding off to order her some refreshment. It was a task he had made a habit of while they'd been on the yacht. The boat might need a sizeable complement of crew to keep it running as smoothly and efficiently as it did, but Jemma rarely ever saw any of them. As with his home in London, Leon liked to be alone to relax. Servants, staff, crew—call them what you like, they irritated him. And she had a suspicion that, if it were possible, he would have sailed this yacht single-handed just to maintain his desire for privacy.

He came back carrying a tray bearing her usual jug of freshly squeezed orange juice and a tall frosted glass, but by then Jemma was over at the rail, gazing out at the scenery going by them.

'I thought you might enjoy a change,' he answered her question as he came to lean beside her. 'So, we are making for a small fishing village called Fiskárdho on the northern tip of Kefallinía—the largest island in the Ionian group,' he explained informatively, 'where I think we will spend what is left of the day doing what any normal tourist would do and browse around the shops, maybe eat dinner in one of the local tavernas—would you like that, *agape mou*?'

'Sounds great!' She lifted smiling eyes to him.

'Good,' he nodded, and drew her attention to the view.

They were moving smoothly through a narrow stretch of deep blue water between two huge misted blocks of land.

'What are they?' she asked, curious because, other than that rushed journey from Corfu airport to pick up the yacht three weeks ago, they had steered well clear of the bigger islands in the group, calling only at the smallest mainly uninhabited islands where tourists rarely went.

'Kefallinía on the left and Ithaki—you might know it as Ithaca—to our right,' he informed her.

'Ithaca?' she cried. 'The island of Homer and the *Odyssey*. How wonderful!' She turned a wistful gaze on the man beside her. 'You're so lucky to be a part of all of this! The legends, the sheer romance of it! I'm jealous,' she confessed.

'Then dare I make another admission?' Leon mused out loud. 'This is my homeland,' he announced. 'I was born here.'

'On Ithaca?' she gasped out enviously.

'No.' Ruefully he shook his dark head. 'I am afraid I cannot make that particularly romantic claim. I am Kefallinían,' he explained. 'And remember how I said that,' he warned. 'Because when we land there Kefalliníans do not like to be called Greek!'

'But the island belongs to Greece!' she protested.

He nodded in agreement. 'But the Irish are Irish, the Scots are Scots and the Welsh are Welsh,' he made the comparison. 'I am Kefallinían.'

'Not Greek,' she said mock-solemnly but her eyes were twinkling.

'Not Greek,' he confirmed with equal mock-solemnity.

'So I didn't marry a Greek tycoon.'

'You married a Kefallinían tycoon,' he corrected.

'Leon Stephanades, the Kefallinían tycoon,' she said frowningly, trying the words out for taste. 'It doesn't have quite as good a ring to it, does it?'

He was trying not to smile. 'Wondering if you'd made a bad mistake marrying me?'

'Well...' Jemma turned to lean her elbows against the rail behind her, totally unconscious of the curving grace of her swollen body '...a girl has to consider her social standing, doesn't she? How much is a Kefallinían tycoon worth?' she quizzed.

'This one is worth—enough,' he answered with a smile.

'Enough for what?' she enquired provocatively.

He laughed, the sound warm and huskily alive. He lifted his hand so that he could take hold of her chin, giving it a playful shake. 'Enough to keep you in luxury for the rest of your beautiful life,' he said, and kissed her.

It was a surprise—enough of a surprise to keep her own mouth still beneath his, her eyes wide and startled when he drew away to look into them. 'You are happier now?' he asked. 'The feelings of homesickness have faded?'

'Yes,' she assured him, smiling apologetically. 'It was a few moments' silliness, that's all, gone before I woke up from my rest.'

His eyes glinted darkly in the sunlight while he explored her face for a few moments longer, then he said quietly, 'You must trust me, Jemma, to do what is right for us. I am both your home and your family now. I do not intend to desert you or play you false.'

'I do trust you,' she said, and surprised herself because she meant it. 'And I'm sorry if my mood upset you.'

'Not upset exactly, but concerned me rather.' He lifted a hand to her hair, gently touching the silky roots at her temple. 'We may have embarked on this marriage because of the coming child, but I never stopped caring for you, Jemma; you must also remember that.'

His words warmed a special place inside her, and she smiled up at him. 'I remember,' she confirmed.

And he had cared, cared enough to ask her to go live with him in New York. Cared enough to marry her when he came back to find her pregnant with his child. And he had cared enough to spend the last few weeks personally supervising her recovery to good health in the most luxurious and pleasurable way he could think of. But——

But what? she asked herself impatiently as she turned her attention back to the view slipping lazily by them.

But caring wasn't enough, she answered herself bleakly. Not any more—not ever, probably. But perhaps more so now because she had become so wholly dependent on him for everything.

CHAPTER NINE

FISKÁRDHO sat at the end of a narrow inlet, its rich blue waters protected by mountains on either side. Because of the size of the yacht, they had to anchor just outside the tiny harbour itself, and within minutes the crew had launched the small speed-boat, Leon had helped her climb down into it and they were speeding across the water towards a pretty hamlet of whitewashed buildings with red-tiled roofs.

It was a busy little place; sailing yachts of all shapes and sizes floated side by side along the two-sided harbour wall. Leon nudged them in between a tall-masted sailing yacht and an expensive-looking motor cruiser, then called out to a small white-haired man who came ambling across to catch the rope Leon threw to him. The two men chatted amiably in Greek while they made the boat safe, then, with an ease that surprised her, Leon picked her up and placed her neatly on the quay before making the two-foot leap to the quayside himself.

Jemma pushed her sunhat off her head so that it hung down her back on its strings and she could look interestedly around her. The little Greek man looked at her hair and said something to Leon who grinned and answered and the man gave a nod of approval and shook Leon's hand.

'What did he say?' she asked curiously.

'He was complimenting me on my taste,' Leon replied.

'And what did you say to him?'

'I told him I was Kefallinían,' he shrugged. 'Of course I had good taste.'

'Conceited devil,' she said.

He just grinned carelessly. 'What would you like to do first?' he asked.

'Stop my body from floating,' she said ruefully. 'I feel as if I'm still on water!'

'It will take a while to get your balance,' he warned. 'Would you rather we sit down and have a drink or something, while you get your land legs back?'

'No.' Jemma's eyes were already darting eagerly around her. 'I haven't seen a shop in weeks, and I want to browse.'

'I thought you might say that,' he sighed. 'Come on, we will begin at one end and work our way to the other. Oh,' he added belatedly, 'this is for you.' He pulled a thick roll of banknotes from his pocket and handed them to her. 'Drachmas,' he explained. 'You will need them if you want to buy anything.'

Jemma bit pensively down on her bottom lip, her reluctance to take the money showing in the expression she could not keep off her face.

'Good grief!' Leon sighed, reading the expression for exactly what it was. 'I have never known a woman like you who will not even accept the simplest offering from her own husband! Take it—take it!' he insisted impatiently, thrusting it into her hands.

'But how much is here?' she demanded suspiciously. It looked an awful lot of money to her.

'The equivalent of a few English pounds only,' he dismissed, watching her grudgingly push the roll into the pocket of her baggy white trousers. 'Now can we go?' he mocked.

She let him lead the way through the crush of people packing the quayside towards the little shops lined up on the other side of the quay, where she soon forgot to be uncomfortable about him giving her money as her eyes began to feast on the array of interesting touristy goods for sale.

They explored the tiny hamlet together, moving in and out of shops which were little more than the front rooms of private houses that had been converted for the season and would, Leon told her, revert back to their original use for the winter months. It was an enchantingly pretty place, and, Jemma realised, rather an up-market one, going by the quality of the produce on show. She went into raptures when they happened to stroll through the narrow door of one shop and she found herself literally tented in the most beautiful hand-made lacework, crochetwork, and exquisite embroidery. She lost Leon almost immediately, becoming immersed in a veritable maze of hung linen. When he eventually found her, she was standing fingering a beautifully crocheted baby shawl. He recognised what it was immediately and she blushed because, although they had married because of the child she carried, other than discussing her own health they rarely mentioned the child itself.

'You want it?' Leon asked her softly.

Jemma nodded, her eyes unknowingly vulnerable when she lifted them to him. 'Do I have enough drachmas to buy it?' she asked uncertainly. 'Only it's hand-made and looks very expensive...'

But Leon was already reaching for the delicate garment, his hands appearing big and dark against the soft white lacework as he unhooked it from its hanger then gravely presented it to her, draping it over her arms—carefully, as though their baby were already wrapped inside it, then stood back, something so intense about the look in his eyes that it caught at Jemma's breath and made their child kick out in protest at the flurry of emotion that rippled through her.

'You are beautiful, do you know that?' he murmured huskily, and bent to kiss her.

He paid for the shawl with his Visa card and had it wrapped in tissue paper and placed in a plastic carrier bag which he then solemnly presented to Jemma. She took it blushingly, feeling unaccountably shy all of a sudden.

A new intimacy seemed to grow between them after that. Leon rarely let go of her hand as they continued to wander from shop to shop, and Jemma felt a dire need always to have her body within brushing distance with his. Her senses began to buzz, and she knew by the new darkened look in his eyes when he looked at her that Leon was feeling the same thing too.

Darkness came around eight o'clock and they decided to make for one of the busy harbourside tavernas, sitting at a rickety old table on severely uncomfortable chairs. And Jemma found herself studying him curiously as he ordered some freshly caught snapper fish and the usual Greek salad to share. He couldn't often put himself into situations like this one, mingling, eating with tourists, yet, despite the unmistakable air of class about him, he blended in quite comfortably.

The meal came with a basket of fresh crusty bread and a large bowl of salad topped with rich feta cheese anointed with oil and herbs from which Leon broke off bits with his fingers and fed them to her as if it was the most natural thing in the world for him to do. They shared a bottle of wine—well, Jemma was allowed one glass; Leon had the rest. They talked quietly, she asking questions about the island, he answering them with a quiet depth of pride that held her more fascinated than the knowledgeable words he spoke. They watched the endless passage of holidaymakers taking an evening stroll along the harbour wall, and the way the lights danced on the silk dark waters in the harbour. They listened in to other people's conversations, smiling with them when someone made a joke, and Leon translating if the language was strange to her, his knowledge of French, Italian, and even a smattering of Danish both surprising and impressing her.

People talked sailing mostly because Fiskárdho, it seemed, was predominantly a sailing resort. And most remarked at some point or other during the evening on the big luxury yacht anchored just outside the bay, making Jemma blush and Leon grin as they speculated on who owned it, their suggestions ranging from Arab sheikhs to the Italian Mafia.

And through it all Leon was unusually attentive towards her, his fingers hardly ever out of contact with her own where they lay on the table, and his eyes warm and slumbrous on her face.

By the time they'd finished their long, leisurely meal, it was getting late. Leon suggested they return to the yacht, the look in his eyes promising that this new intimacy they were sharing was not going to end on their return. Trembling a little in anticipation, she let him help her to her feet. Their eyes met, and they kissed gently, then his arm was about her shoulders and her hand slid around his waist as they strolled silently back to where they had left the small boat.

The little white-haired man was there to hold the boat steady on its rope while Leon jumped in then reached up to lift her down to join him. Their bodies brushed, sending a sprinkle of awareness skittering through her, and on a soft gasp she looked down and away from his knowing gaze, hiding the sudden heat that rushed into her cheeks.

She trembled all the way back to the yacht where two crew members waited to make safe the little boat and help them board. Leon broke their usual routine by escorting her down to her cabin when usually he stayed on the sun-deck when she came to bed.

A *frisson* of heat tingled through her at the sound of the door closing quietly behind them. She turned to look at him. 'Thank you f-for a lovely...' Evening, she had been about to say, but the look in his eyes dried up her mouth, and she had to look away, her agitated gaze darting around the room in search of something, any-thing she could pretend interest in so long as she didn't have to look at him. Her eyes alighted on her nightdress laid out on the bed and she snatched it up, crushing the soft cotton to her breasts only to gasp when Leon cap-tured her wrist and pulled her around to face him.

'Not tonight, *agape mou*,' he murmured softly, taking the nightdress from her and tossing it aside. 'Not tonight.'

Then he was cupping her face, his fingers threading into the silky thickness of her hair as he urged her to look at him. His eyes were dark and disturbingly alive, transmitting his next intention even before he lowered his head. And it was no passive kiss. It was a hot, hunting kiss that demanded an answering response from her and got it hungrily, her hands snaking up to grasp the sides of his face, holding him, urging him on, her mouth warm and seeking, telling him that she wanted this too.

It had been building up all evening. She had known it even while she'd tried hard to pretend it wasn't there. But now, as his arms slid around her to draw her fully against him, there was no pretending any longer.

Leon wanted to make love to her. Why he had chosen today to change the status quo she had no idea, but it certainly had changed, and she could feel the power of his desire pulsing urgently against her.

He undressed her slowly, his fingers loosening buttons and sliding sensually over her throat, the satin slopes of her breasts, the rounded firmness of her stomach, smothering her soft responding gasps with the passionate crush of his mouth. His hands slid inside the elastic waist of her trousers, drawing the thin fabric downwards with an agonising slowness. She shuddered when he touched her intimately, a crescendo of tight curling pleasure arching her back so that their child pressed against him and her mouth left his so that she could let her head fall backwards on a soft, pleasurable sigh.

His mouth found her breasts, making them sting into tight, painful life and she inhaled on a sharp gasp of air.

'I hurt you?' His head came up, burning black eyes shot through with concern.

'No,' she denied. 'I'm just—sensitive, that's all.' Then on a driven groan, 'Oh, God, Leon. Do it again!'

Her breathless plea seemed to rock him, his own breath crashing from his lungs as he caught her mouth. Her shirt slid from her shoulders to land in a pool at their feet, followed by his shirt, then their naked torsos were together, hot and throbbing. He drew her down to lie on the bed, hands hurriedly removing the rest of their clothes before he joined her, and Jemma was already reaching for him, one arm hooking around his neck while the other hand went for the muscled tightness of his hip, pulling him against her, legs tangling, bodies moving in that hot, sensual rhythm of urgent need.

It had been a long time—too long for both of them if their responses were a measure. His mouth was moist and searching on her breasts, his caresses urgent as he aroused her.

'Will I hurt you?' he asked tensely when it was obvious neither of them could stand much more of it without full, exquisite possession.

'No,' she whispered, and was sure of it. She was ready, her body so supple that it felt boneless in its need. He came over her, his forearms keeping most of his weight from her, but as he carefully thrust himself inside her Jemma let out a frustrated groan and pulled him down on top of her. It wasn't enough just to join. She needed to feel him—all of him, bearing down on her with all the heat and passion she had missed for so long.

Relief came like the slow-motion shattering of glass, bursting out from a central point where the nub of her desire had coiled itself tightly in readiness for this final devastating blast. He went with her; she felt him, heard him, cried out as he cried out, and their bodies blended in a hot fusion of moist flesh and trembling limbs.

Afterwards, he just held her, held her curled closely into the curve of his own body. And when she tried to move he stopped her, hands tightening, mouth brushing a silent plea across her heated cheek. They didn't speak, he didn't seem to want that either, her only attempt cut off with a husky, 'Shh. You belong, *agape mou*. You must feel it now. You belong here with me.' And again the tightening of the arms to stop her when she tried to answer him.

It was a mark, she realised, of how deeply her melancholy earlier had affected him that he needed to keep referring to it. Oh, not just with words, but with the way he had been with her since she woke up this afternoon. More attentive, physically more responsive, in the way he had constantly kept her close to him, touching her—with the caress of his eyes as well as his hands. As if he had realised that the kind of easy friendship they had developed over the last few weeks was not enough for her to feel secure with him, and he wanted her to feel secure. Was that also why he had made love to her just now? she wondered. As a statement of possession, for both of them, because she would have to be stupid not to know that Leon had gained as much from their loving as she had.

Then another thought trickled insidiously into her mind, one which filled her with a purring warmth she had never dared allow herself before. He had already reminded her once today that he cared for her. But then to go to the lengths he had done just to reassure her again? It had to hint at more than caring, more than just a reluctant husband wanting to make the best of his lot.

Could it even be that he was falling just a little bit in love with her?

Jemma sighed wistfully, and burrowed deeper into the circle of his arms, feeling a new level of contentment settle softly over her, and she fell asleep like that, coiled against him, he wrapped around her.

It was very early in the morning when something woke them. A sound that impinged on their subconsciousness and brought Leon alert with a jerk before he was suddenly leaping naked out of the bed. He glanced out of the window, swore, then turned angrily towards the bathroom.

'What is it?' Jemma asked sleepily.

'Nothing,' he muttered. 'Go back to sleep.'

He disappeared through the bathroom door, leaving her lying there frowning in puzzlement at his odd behaviour. Then the noise became louder, and she recognised it as the whirling sound of a helicopter's blades. She listened sleepily as it swooped low over the top of the yacht then whirled away across the surface of the water before coming to a hovering stop somewhere not far away.

Leon came back showered, with a towel draped around his hips. He didn't look at her but bent to recover his clothes still lying where he had tossed them on the floor the night before.

'Is that helicopter bringing someone to see you?' she asked.

'Yes.' The answer was tight and angry.

'But who?' she persisted. Other than the launch which brought him papers daily to the yacht, no one else had tried to see him.

'I cannot tell as yet,' he said. But his angry expression alone said he had a damned good idea. He looked at her at last, that anger flicking at her, until he realised whom he was looking at and he sighed shortly, and came over to sit down on the bed.

'You look beautiful in the morning, do you know that?'

'Flattery will not get you anywhere,' she pouted. 'I want to know what's going on.'

'And you will,' he assured her. 'When I know.' He covered her mouth with his, tasting cleanly of toothpaste and smelling freshly of soap.

Then he was up again, and shrugging into his creased trousers and crumpled shirt. 'Stay there,' he commanded over his shoulder. 'It is still early. Try to get some more sleep if you can. If you cannot, then ring for your breakfast to be served in here.' He turned back to her at that, his expression firm when he added commandingly, 'I want you to remain in here, *agape mou*, until I have got rid of—whoever it is.'

'But why?' she said, puzzled by the command.

'Because your husband asks you to, of course,' he answered arrogantly.

'That is not a good enough reason,' she responded, watching the economical way he made himself look reasonably decent. 'And anyway, how do you know that helicopter was bringing someone to see you? You can't be the only important man on this island. Perhaps it's come to...'

Her voice trailed off, made to by the sound of the speed-boat being lowered into the water. Leon glanced wryly at her, as if that sound said it all. Then he was coming to lean over her and placing another clinging kiss on her lips. 'Do as I ask, please,' he requested. 'It is important to me that you stay in here.'

'All right,' she agreed, but she didn't like the feeling she got that he was hiding her away like some dark and dirty secret.

'Thank you,' he smiled, then kissed the top of her nose and was gone, striding out of the room and firmly closing the door behind him, leaving Jemma feeling hurt and confused.

Surprisingly, she did sleep. She hadn't intended to—but, after lying there for several long minutes listening to the familiar roar of the speed-boat and the scuffling sounds of people boarding the boat, she felt her eyes drooping sleepily, and the next thing she knew she was being disturbed once again by the swishing sound of the helicopter blades swooping low over the yacht as it sped away.

She sat up, struggling to bring her fuzzy mind into focus. Then she remembered, and climbed quickly off the bed to dress and go in search of Leon.

She found him in the main salon, standing with a cup of coffee in his hand staring out of the window. 'I presume I can come out now,' she drawled sarcastically.

He didn't answer or even turn to greet her, and Jemma paused on the threshold of the room, a cold sense of alarm dispersing her sense of injury.

'Leon?' she questioned anxiously. 'Is something wrong?'

He made an effort to pull himself together. 'Of course not,' he said, turning to smile at her. 'Actually,' he added, 'we have been invited to a party tonight.'

'A party?' She blinked, not understanding the mixed vibrations she was receiving from him. One set warned her he was furiously angry about something, and the other set were saying he was as relaxed as any man could be.

'Yes. A birthday party to be exact. Have you had breakfast?' he enquired suddenly. She shook her head. 'Then I will order you something.' Smoothly he walked over to the telephone and punched in the number which would connect him with the galley. 'Inside or on the sun-deck?' he asked.

She blinked, shaking her head in confusion. 'I... Here, I think,' she decided absently, wishing she could work out what was going on here, because she was sure that something was. 'Whose birthday party is it?' she asked him frowningly.

There was a distinct pause before he answered though he tried to cover it up by making the most of replacing the telephone receiver and straightening the twisted cord. Then, 'My father's,' he informed her.

His father's? A sudden thought hit her. 'Leon, y-your father does know about me, doesn't he? Th-that we're married and I am—pregnant?'

Another pause. Then, 'No,' he told her, 'he doesn't know about you—or the child.' That stiff smile touched his mouth again. 'So you will both come as a—pleasant surprise to him tonight, won't you?'

Will we? Jemma sank heavily into a chair, that feeling of dread emulsifying. She was remembering the Greek girl from the wealthy family Cassie had once mentioned, and knew without a doubt that, far from being a pleasant surprise for his father, she was going to be the complete opposite.

'I don't want to go,' she said dully.

'And why not? I thought you wanted to know about my family,' he reminded her, adding drily, 'Well, tonight you will get your chance.'

But Jemma shook her head. 'No,' she repeated. 'Not like this. Not just dumped on them with no prior warning. It wouldn't be fair, not on them, not on me. I won't do it.' She shook her head. 'Go on your own, if you like, Leon, but I shall remain here on the yacht, if you don't mind.'

'But I do mind,' he drawled, and suddenly that hard, cool core in him that he rarely ever turned on her was very evident in the air. She looked up, saw the intractable expression on his face, and her heart sank. He was standing across the room, leaning against the window-frame, but he might as well have been sitting behind his desk in an office somewhere on the other side of the world for the distance she suddenly felt between them.

'You are my wife now, Jemma,' he reminded her. 'And as my wife you will accompany me to my father's house tonight and be presented to him as such.'

'And the woman your father had already picked out for you to marry?' she cried. 'Will she be there, also?'

Surprise flickered in his eyes, followed by almost instant comprehension. 'Cassie, I presume,' he drawled. Then, on a sigh, 'All right,' he conceded. 'So, it is not going to be a—pleasant evening. But whatever happens there tonight, *agape mou*, none of it is going to change a single thing for us.'

'You're sure about that?' Her voice sounded uncertain and pleaded for reassurance. 'What if your father throws you out on your ear for marrying yourself to the likes of me?'

Leon actually laughed at that, albeit harshly. 'I can positively assure you, my darling, that on meeting you, throwing me out will be the last thing on my father's mind!'

CHAPTER TEN

THEN why do I feel a bit as the lamb must feel when being led off for the slaughter? Jemma wondered miserably hours later as she stood in her bathrobe, staring at the several beautiful evening gowns Leon had provided for her, hating every one of them. 'Or worse,' she muttered, 'as if I'm about to attend my own wake?'

'Did you say something?'

Leon appeared at the half-open door, already dressed in an exquisitely cut taupe linen suit and a loose-fitting cream shirt left open at the throat to reveal the rich brown skin. He looked sleek and expensive and so darned attractive that her mouth went dry, her senses, just like the first time she'd ever set eyes on him, veering madly off course.

'You're not dressed!' he proclaimed the absolute obvious.

'Nothing fits!' she snapped, her eyes sparkling the threat of war if he wasn't careful. 'What use is all this—couture elegance to me——' she waved a scornful hand at the outfits which had been delivered to the yacht barely an hour ago '—when I'm six months pregnant and blown up like a stupid balloon?'

'Have you tried any of them on?' His voice sounded velvet-smooth in contrast to her shrill onslaught.

'Why bother?' she derided, moving to sit down on the dressing-stool. She stretched her bare feet out in front of her and stared mulishly at them. 'I just know they won't fit.'

Leon studied her in silence for a moment, seeing what to him what must look like a silly pregnant woman having

140

a temperamental fit! When really she was just plain frightened. She did not want to go. She had, in fact, turned so chicken inside that she was actually shaking like a leaf.

'*Agape mou*——' he walked further into the room '—I had these clothes flown in specially from Athens——'

'I know that!' she responded scornfully.

Couture dresses from couture houses with couture labels stitched inside, transported from Athens to Argostólion by special courier on one of the Stephanades private planes! She hadn't even known they owned their own planes until she'd discovered how the dresses arrived. Just as she hadn't realised—thick, stupid fool that she was—just how wealthy a family she had married herself into until she'd seen the stir they caused when they sailed into the island's capital of Argostólion this afternoon.

'It doesn't mean they will fit,' she reiterated glumly.

'Maternity clothes,' Leon said quietly.

'What?' Her chin came off her chest so that she could stare at him.

He sighed impatiently. 'I may be a mere man,' he mocked, 'but I do have some sense. These are garments specially designed for a woman in your condition.'

He was not mere anything, Jemma thought peevishly as she slid her eyes back to the four dresses hanging on the outside of the wardrobe. They didn't look like maternity wear. One was a slinky blue thing that looked from here as if it poured itself down to the ground. The next was short straight and black, and she knew, because she'd looked, that it had no back in it whatsoever. The red one was pure Ginger Rogers with a gathered layer of fine georgette over a satin underdress. And the last one was white, short and strapless, made in an unusual fabric that was soft and stretchy and as light as air—and looked as though it would fit her rather like an elastic tube would—hiding nothing.

None of them was suitable. 'Specially designed or not,' she grunted, 'I would rather wear one of your shirts than any of them.'

'Fine,' Leon said, deliberately, she suspected, taking the wind out of her bad-tempered sails. 'If that is what you will feel most comfortable in, then wear one.' He shrugged as if he didn't care less. 'But make up your mind quickly because the car will be here in ten minutes to pick us up.'

'Chauffeur-driven, I presume,' she jeered.

'Jemma!' He sighed. 'What is the matter with you?' He glanced at his watch, solid gold and glinting against his dark brown wrist. 'You have done nothing but mock me since we arrived here this afternoon! What have I done to deserve it?'

'Nothing,' she mumbled, and he hadn't—not really. If anything, Leon had been as pleasant and attentive as a man could be since he'd told her about tonight. Soothing her into a false sense of security, that bitchy voice in her head taunted. She let out a short sigh of defeat, and looked uncertainly back at the dresses. 'You choose,' she told him. 'I'm just too nervous to make up my mind.'

He looked about to argue, his good mood ruined by her peevish manner. Then he saw the honest anxiety in her deep blue eyes and sighed heavily. 'Jemma, you have to trust me. I won't let them lay a single finger on you.'

'Maybe not,' she agreed. 'But you can't stop them looking at me as though I were a rogue cow who's just run off with their prize bull!'

'Prize bull, am I?' He grinned, sharp even teeth gleaming white between his attractive lips. 'Then you had better wear the red,' he decided ruefully.

Jemma looked at the red, then shook her head. 'It's long and it must be thirty degrees out there. I'll be too hot in it.'

'Which therefore cuts out the blue, also,' he said, 'which leaves only the black or the white.'

'I don't want to wear black.' She would really feel as if she was going to a wake in black. 'And the white one is too—clingy-looking. They'll know at a glance why you married me if I wore that!'

Silence. Jemma wasn't sure what she had just said to make him react like that, but Leon was suddenly very still and very grim-faced. She soon found out. 'Are you ashamed, by any chance, of the fact that you carry our child?' he questioned silkily.

'No!' she denied. 'Of course I'm not!'

'Ashamed of me, then?' he suggested.

'Don't be stupid, Leon!' she scoffed. 'Why should I be ashamed of you?'

'Then it has to be yourself you are ashamed of,' he decided, walking towards her with a mood about him that had her jumping warily to her feet.

'I'm not ashamed of anything!' she snapped as he reached out and took hold of her upper arms.

'Good,' he said. 'Because no wife of mine has anything to be ashamed of, do you hear?' He gave her a small shake. 'And neither does she have to hide the evidence of our lovemaking as if it were some dirty secret!'

She winced visibly at his cutting words, but found she could not deny there was a hint of truth in them.

Letting go of her, he moved away, his back stiff with anger. 'Be ready to leave in ten minutes or be sure, Jemma,' he threatened, 'I shall come and dress you myself!'

She wore the white, and was surprised to discover that, far from clinging to every generous curve of her, it had a clever cut to it that made it skim rather flatteringly. She left her hair down, mainly because it gave her greater confidence to feel the long, twisting waves brushing against the sun-kissed skin of her shoulders. And, on impulse, she added a second protection, with a large white silk-fringed shawl which she draped around her shoulders.

Leon was standing by the salon window frowning out at the pitch-black night, but he turned when he heard her come in, then went still, his eyes dark and appraising as they ran slowly over her from her white strappy mules to the free-flowing richness of her sun-streaked hair.

'Beautiful,' he said simply, and held out his hands in a 'what else can I say?' kind of compliment that warmed her all the way through. Then he was coming towards her, a sudden sober expression on his face.

'I have something I want you to wear for me,' he murmured, producing a flat velvet box from his pocket. 'They will expect to see it,' he explained, and flicked open the lid.

Jemma stared down at it, and felt an odd chill clutch at her heart. It was a necklace. Big and conspicuous, almost gaudy with its huge sparkling diamonds surrounded by rich dark rubies. Priceless it had to be; she did not even think of questioning its authenticity. But it was ugly to the point that she actually shuddered, and was relieved when Leon said drily, 'I know, it's awful. But it was my mother's and they will expect to see it on you—even though it was a well known fact that she hated it too.'

His mother's. Somehow hearing that changed her whole impression of the necklace. 'Did your father give it to her?' she asked with sudden insight.

'Yes.' Leon's smile was wry. 'Says a lot for his taste, doesn't it? It was his first big social mistake and he's going to hate being reminded of it when he sees it on you—if you'll wear it for me, that is.'

'You like riling him, don't you?' Jemma noted drily.

'Love it,' he admitted. 'You see, he married my mother simply to get his hands on the Leonadis fortune, then proceeded to make her life hell until the day she died.'

Oh, my, Jemma thought as suddenly lots of missing pieces from the puzzle began to slot neatly into place. So, the Leonadis Corporation had belonged to his mother's family and not his father. It had never occurred to her to question the reason for the two different names.

'And your brother?' she asked. 'Where does he fit into all of this?'

'Half-brother,' he corrected. 'Nico was born just eight months after my father remarried, which was six months after my mother died.'

'How old were you?' she questioned gently.

'Eight.' He paused, a sudden flash of pain hitting his features. 'Anthia was my father's mistress before and during his marriage to my mother,' he said, then added flatly, 'She wanted everything my mother had—even this necklace.'

'I'll wear it,' Jemma said, and accepted the kiss he pressed to her forehead for what it was—a thank-you for her understanding.

'Turn around and hold up your hair.'

She did so reluctantly, shivering as the cold, heavy necklace came to rest against her warm skin. She looked down at it, seeing the way the jewels flashed in the overhead light. 'I feel as gaudy as a Christmas tree,' she complained.

Leon kissed her exposed nape. 'I promise to replace it with something more tasteful at the first opportunity I get,' he vowed, settling her hair back about her sun-kissed shoulders. 'In fact,' he added as he turned her to face him again, 'I never did get you that special gift in return for the one you gave to me.' His mouth went ruefully awry, as though he did not like himself much for the omission. 'I owe you, *agape mou*. I——'

'But you did give me my gift, Leon,' she inserted softly. 'A beautiful gift. One I wouldn't change for the world.' Taking hold of his hand, she laid it tenderly on their child.

His eyes went black, emotion burning up from somewhere deep inside him, then he was pulling her into his arms. He didn't kiss her, but just held her very close for a moment, and Jemma felt tears sting at the back of her eyes because she knew she had just unwittingly reached in and touched a very vulnerable part of him.

'I do not deserve you,' he murmured as he drew away.

'Mmm,' she agreed, teasing him with the gentle humour in her eyes.

Yet, rather than making him smile with her, if anything he looked suddenly angry. His hands tightened on her shoulders. 'Jemma,' he said impulsively. 'I——' Then he stopped himself, impatience straightening the softer line of his mouth. 'Let's go,' he muttered instead, his mood dark with purpose as he led the way off the yacht to where a dark limousine was waiting at the bottom of the companionway.

A white-uniformed chauffeur jumped to open the rear door for them. Leon saw Jemma inside then joined her, the mask of cool sophistication she only ever saw him wear when they were in others' company slipping smoothly into place now.

They didn't speak, and Jemma fixed her attention on what was going on beyond the car window as they flashed smoothly by invitingly lit tavernas and bars with their tables packed with scantily dressed holidaymakers who looked tanned and happy and relaxed.

As they must have looked last night, she thought wistfully, wishing they were back in Fiskárdho wearing the casual clothes of the tourist and enjoying a simple meal in congenial company.

Last night had been one of the sweetest she'd ever spent—mainly because Leon had made it that way. Tonight promised to be the opposite in every way.

Leaving the main part of the town behind them, they began to climb through residential suburbs then out into a starlit countryside. To their right, the sea shone like billowing black silk with the silvered light of the moon on it. And she could just make out the dark bulk of land on the other side of the water curving like an elephant's trunk around the Gulf of Argostólion.

'Lassi,' Leon murmured when her face lit with interest as they dropped into sudden bright, busy life again. 'It is the main holiday resort on the island, because of the good sandy beaches here.'

'It looks very lively,' she remarked, her voice unknowingly wistful.

'Hmm,' was all he said to that. 'My father's villa is not far from here,' he told her instead.

That brought back her tension, and she sat quietly beside him as they turned off the main road, taking a narrow lane that went beneath a canopy of trees which made it difficult to see much after that, with no streetlights to ease the darkness, until they slowed suddenly and turned in through a stone-arched gateway. And she felt her tension increase when she saw the rows of expensive cars lining the wide driveway where the two-storey building at the end of it looked more like a medium-sized hotel than a private home.

The car came to a stop at the bottom of a set of shallow steps which led up to the wide arched doorway where two white-shirted servants stood waiting to receive the guests.

The chauffeur jumped out of the car to open the rear door for them. But when Jemma went to alight, Leon laid a hand on her arm and shook his head. 'Wait,' he said, and climbed out on the other side, coming around to help her alight himself.

It was an oddly courteous gesture and one which warmed her even if it did nothing to ease the nervous tension from her stiffened limbs as she walked beside him.

The two doormen jerked to attention as they walked in, by the respectful looks on their faces, recognising Leon instantly. He ignored them with that arrogance which used to annoy her, but she was beginning to read it better now, and see it for the defence mechanism it was to him.

Leon was not at all comfortable being here in his father's house. Not that it would show to anyone else, she noted as she kept pace with his smooth, easy stride with his arm comfortingly warm around her waist.

The entrance hall was big and luxurious, with a pure white marble floor and modern black furniture set against white walls. It led right through from the front to the back of the house, and by the emptiness of the rooms either side of them Jemma had to assume that the party was taking place elsewhere, which proved to be outside, as she realised when Leon led her down the marble hallway towards the growing hum of chatter coming from the garden beyond the open rear doors.

They were late. It took Jemma just ten seconds to realise it as they paused on the threshold to look out on the subtly lit garden where—at a quick and frightening guess—about one hundred people sat around the tables set upon a large paved area in front of a circular swimming-pool.

Not just late, but rudely late, she realised, when she noticed the coffee-cups and liqueur glasses on the table. And deliberately so if she was reading Leon accurately.

As if picking up on her thoughts, he murmured softly, 'It looks as though we have timed it just right.'

But before she had time to ponder on this last cryptic remark someone noticed them, and the woman's surprised gasp brought all heads turning in their direction.

It was amazing how total silence could deafen, Jemma thought as she felt her body go heavy with dread. She slipped her hand beneath Leon's jacket and clutched at a fistful of his soft linen shirt.

'Easy,' he soothed her quietly. But Jemma could feel the tension in him. He was as uptight as she was.

'So, you deign to arrive at last.'

Two things hit her at that moment: one, that the voice which spoke was harsh and angry, and the other that it spoke in English, which surprised her. The anger did not.

Leon's father, it had to be, she assumed, because the man just rising to his feet was simply an older version of the man standing beside her. On his right sat the most exquisitely beautiful woman with the coldest pair of black eyes Jemma had ever seen, and on her right reclined a young man who could only be Leon's half-brother because, again, he looked so incredibly like him—except for the thinness of his mouth. That had a slightly peevish look about it, and cold, like the woman he sat beside.

It was then she saw the two empty places on the other side of Leon's father, and felt a wave of embarrassment wash over her. Those had to have been their places for dinner.

'Father.' Beside her, Leon acknowledged the other man with a smooth nod. 'Many happy returns for your birthday.'

His father's mouth tightened angrily. 'Is that all you are going to say?' he demanded.

'No.' Leon nudged Jemma into movement. She didn't want to go, so he had to exert pressure to her shoulders to make her, and she found herself walking on shaking legs towards the clutch of tables. 'I wish you many more of them,' he added politely.

There was one small comfort, she noted tensely as she felt the prickling sting of one hundred pairs of eyes pierce

her. No one had noticed her condition yet, simply because their eyes were locked on the awful necklace
gleaming between the fringed folds of her otherwise
concealing shawl.

A great diversion, she acknowledged half hysterically,
her fingers taking an even tighter grip on that precious
piece of shirt she was clinging to as a whisper of gasps
and murmurs skittered around the garden. The woman
seated beside Leon's father was staring at Jemma's throat
in something close to horror, his half-brother stiffening
in his seat. Yet no one spoke—no one seemed daring
enough—as Leon guided them between their tables and
chairs until he came to a stop beside his father, his arm
resting across her trembling shoulders.

The older man had been staring at the necklace too,
but now his glance flicked up to clash with his son's.
There was a question in his eyes—and a strange touch
of excitement that Jemma did not understand. He
seemed to swallow rather thickly. 'Is this——?'

He was interrupted, not by Leon, but by the woman
sitting to his father's right. 'We expected you at seven,
Leon,' she censured, coming stiffly to her feet. She was
tall and incredibly slender—and with an aristocratic
manner about her that put Jemma in awe. She flashed
the necklace a hard look, but other than that honed her
cold eyes exclusively on Leon. 'It is now gone nine
o'clock!'

There was another moment's short, sharp silence while
Leon continued to hold his father's gaze, strange mes-
sages, Jemma sensed, flashing from one man to the
other, then he flicked his eyes to the other woman.
'Anthia,' he acknowledged. 'As beautiful as ever, I see.'

She did not take the remark as a compliment, her cold
face stiffening. And it was only then, and at such close
quarters to her, that Jemma realised that she had to be
in her late fifties. It was just that she had cared for her

body and face through the years, and it had paid off, because there was hardly an age-line on her.

'Were you deliberately trying to ruin your father's birthday?' she demanded. 'Does he not even get an apology from you for your rudeness?'

Leon leaned forward a little, the eye-to-eye contact between the two of them a formidable force in itself. 'Does my companion get an apology for the way you are deliberately ignoring her?' he threw back softly.

Jemma stiffened up like a board, even her chin going rigid on a complete overload of stress.

Again, the woman's eyes flicked to the necklace, and something close to panic spoiled their soulless expression before she was coolly back in control again. 'Since it is you who are so rudely late,' she drawled, 'I therefore think your... companion will understand why your introductions will have to wait until after we have finished here.' She made a gesture towards their listening audience with a long, languidly graceful white hand. 'As you very well know,' she went on tightly, 'your father is about to make an important announcement, and we would appreciate it if you would at least show some manners, and let him get on with it.'

Another moment's taut silence while Leon held the other woman's angry gaze. Then, 'But of course, Anthia, you are quite right,' he conceded with a sudden backdown from the confrontation that everyone, even Jemma, had felt brewing. 'Father must be allowed to continue—no matter what,' he agreed. 'But first I am afraid I really must show my poor manners yet again, and insist on making my own small announcement. *Agape mou*,' he murmured, drawing Jemma closer to his side, 'I would like you to meet my father, Dimitri Stephanades. Father,' he continued softly, 'my beautiful wife, Jemma.'

Stunned silence. It drummed in her ears. Dry-mouthed—terrified how she would be received—Jemma lifted her eyes to Dimitri Stephanades's, the tension so fraught inside her that she could feel her blood-pressure rising perilously. Leon's hand tightened on her shoulder as if to give her courage, and she swallowed nervously, her dry tongue sweeping around her parched lips as she forced a trembling hand upwards to offer it tentatively to the older version of Leon.

How it happened she was never sure, whether by accident or design. But as she lifted her arm, Leon shifted his resting arm, catching her shawl so that the fine silk slithered from her shoulders and fell in a whisper to the floor.

An audible gasp shot around the garden, the necklace losing its impact as all eyes honed in on her obvious state of pregnancy. Someone knocked over a drink, the glass splintering noisily as it smashed against a wine bottle. Someone else giggled, a nervous sound that was cut off as acutely as it had begun. And Jemma stood, paralysed and feeling utterly exposed, as Leon's father went perfectly white, his eyes fixed unblinkingly on her body.

Then Leon was saying in a tight commanding whisper, 'Take her hand, Father. Welcome your new daughter into the family.'

Dimitri Stephanades jerked his eyes back to his son's. There was definite shock written there and something else Jemma could not interpret but knew that, whatever it was, it went very deep. Then he swallowed, and said something hoarsely in Greek. Leon nodded. 'Most definitely mine!' he said with a fierce driving possessiveness. 'My child. My *son*!' he added triumphantly. 'I have seen him living and moving with my own eyes!'

Shock hit her broadside, closing her eyes and draining her face of the last vestige of colour, sending her outstretched hand dropping to her side where it clenched into a tight, trembling fist. A son. Leon knew their child was a boy, and her mind flicked back to the day they had visited the doctor and Leon had slipped away to speak to him privately while Jemma got dressed again. The doctor had asked while they watched the scan of their child whether they wished to know its sex, and Jemma had said no, firmly, because she wanted to enjoy the element of surprise.

Now Leon had spoiled that forever, and in front of one hundred witnesses. Ruthless she knew him to be, or he would not be the formidable force he was to the business world. Angry with his father she had known. But this angry—this ruthless, that he would use her as some kind of weapon that was at this very moment causing some great chain reaction among the murmuring crowd, and that he had destroyed forever her trust in him?

She wanted to turn and run, get out of here and away from all these people and their little power games—because she was in no doubt that it was a struggle for power that was taking place right now—but her legs would not allow her to move. They were stiff and tingling with the imminent threat of completely collapsing beneath her and she knew the only thing that was holding her upright was Leon's arm—treacherous though it was—clamped about her thickened waist.

Someone tried to say something, her voice sharp with shock. But Leon's father waved her into silence. It was Leon's stepmother, her black eyes glazed with horror as she sank heavily back into her chair. Then Dimitri Stephanades was looking pleadingly at his eldest son.

Leon did not move, neither physically nor emotionally. 'You have an announcement to make,' he reminded him. 'I suggest you do it—then we talk, I think.'

It was so obviously the conditional terms of a victor to the defeated that it seemed decidedly odd, even to Jemma's totally stunned mind, that his father's eyes should suddenly look fire-bright with what she could only describe as elation.

'Of course,' he agreed, and almost dutifully turned to face the silenced party.

'As you all no doubt know,' he began smoothly enough, 'today I reached my sixty-fifth year, and the doctors, wise men that they are, have advised me it is time to abdicate my throne and go tend my vines.' A ripple of nervous laughter skittered around the garden. 'Let no one think it is an easy thing to accept that I am getting too old to maintain control of what has been my life's work, for it is not,' he confessed. 'But, for my own health's sake—and the sake of the Leonadis Corporation—I have decided to hand over the reins of power into more—capable hands.' His tone alone said he was doing so reluctantly. 'I have two sons,' he continued flatly, 'both of whom I am undoubtedly proud of, both equally capable of reigning supreme in my place. I therefore had a choice,' he explained. 'To split the company into two and give them one half each, or do what any wise businessman should do and keep the company strong in unity. I chose unity,' he informed the listening throng. 'Consequently, several weeks ago I had drawn up a legal document, laying down the grounds on which either son could ascend into my place. It involved several points I considered necessary before I would hand my life's work over to their care, the most important of these being, of course, the continuance of the Stephanades line. I therefore made this proviso...' He paused and took in a breath of air. 'The first of them to provide me with the grandson I so much desire will take my place as chairman of the Leonadis Corporation. This, of course, was to be the nucleus of my announcement tonight but——' the twisted smile appeared again '—as you can all see, my son Leonadis has preempted me. So...' he lifted his eyes, sending them on a cool scan of his rapt audience, then picked up the half-filled champagne glass standing in front of him '...please stand and raise your glasses to Leon and his wife—

Jemma...' The name fell stiltedly off his tongue. 'And, because Leon informs me it is so and I have never had any reason to doubt his word, my as yet unborn grandson. I therefore announce Leon as my immediate successor. *Yássas*!' he concluded, and drank.

Silence—it was both spectacular and nullifying. Then the place seemed to erupt as a hundred people came to their feet, and while Jemma stood, numbed through to the very core of her being by the depth of Leon's usage of her, they raised their glasses and said, '*Yássas*!' just as she sank into a deep, dark faint.

CHAPTER ELEVEN

JEMMA came around slowly, the sound of voices raised in anger and the blurred impression that she was not going to like what she was coming back to keeping her sunk in a semi-conscious haze. She vaguely recalled Leon carrying her inside the house and laying her gently on something smooth and soft, but other than that she did not remember—and did not want to.

'But this is madness, Dimitri!' a shrill voice suddenly cried, high-pitched and impossible to ignore. 'We know nothing about this woman—or the child she carries! It could well not even be Leon's child!'

'Are you suggesting I am a fool, Anthia?' From much, much closer, Leon's voice was quiet but deadly grim.

'No. But I am suggesting that you would sink to anything to grab full power!'

'Including claiming another man's child as my own, it seems.'

'And why not?' the cold voice challenged. 'It is all a little too convenient, is it not? After all, who is she? What is she? Why is it that we knew nothing of her existence until tonight?'

'She is my wife,' Leon stated harshly. 'The rest is none of your business!'

'It is if this is just a deliberate ploy to disinherit your brother!'

'Half-brother,' Leon corrected. 'There is a subtle but fundamental difference. The Leonadis Corporation belonged to my mother, not his.'

'Enough,' another deep voice commanded. 'This has gone far enough! Leon, you will remember, please, that

156

the Leonadis company is mine, regardless of its origin. And you, Anthia, will not imply that Leon is a cheat. He is my son, and his loyalty to me has always been unimpeachable.'

'Until tonight,' Dimitri's wife could not resist adding.

God, thought Jemma, she could taste the bitterness and hostility. It sickened her, turned her stomach and made her wonder just what she had been thrust into here.

She moved, struggling to push herself into a sitting position, and brought an icy hand up to cover her clammy brow.

'Jemma.' Leon was beside her in an instant, squatting down to bring his face at a level with her own. He looked grim and anxious, his eyes raking over her colourless face. Behind him Jemma could see the small clutch of stiff and angry people eyeing her grimly from the other side of the room. 'How do you feel?' he murmured concernedly. 'Any pain, discomfort? I grabbed you quite roughly when you fainted. And you have been out a long time.' Frowning, he reached out to brush a stray lock of hair from her ice-cold cheek. 'It concerned me enough to call the doctor,' he informed her. 'He will be here soon.'

'Safeguarding your interests, Leon?' she jeered, shrugging his hand away.

His mouth tightened, but he did not retaliate, studying her frowningly instead, calculating the extent of her physical distress, the emotional one already self-evident.

A glass of water appeared in front of her and she went to wave it away, but a soft female voice urged, 'Drink; it will help.' And she looked up to find herself staring into the kindest face she had seen here tonight. Older than herself, the woman was smiling encouragingly. Jemma took the glass, but her fingers were shaking so badly that she couldn't drink from it, and the woman closed her own warmer fingers around Jemma's and gently helped the glass to her lips. She was glad she was

there, glad because her elegant figure effectively blocked
Jemma off from the rest of the room, and glad because
it meant she did not have to concentrate on the man
squatting in front of her.

A few tentative sips at the cool water, and Jemma felt
her rocked senses begin to settle. She smiled her thanks
at the woman and let her take the glass from her.

'Jemma——'

'Don't speak to me!' she flashed.

The woman looked surprised as though she couldn't
believe anyone would dare speak to Leon Stephanades
in that tone. 'You have found your ideal match, I see,'
she drawled mockingly to Leon.

'More than my match,' he said with a tight forced
smile. 'She beats me with her broomstick twice a week.'

'Be careful I don't decide to turn you into a snake!'
Jemma snapped.

The woman laughed, and so did Leon, but there was
a moment's angry flash in his eyes that said he had more
than understood her acid meaning. Then he sighed
heavily and lowered his gaze to where he had his hands
clenched between his bent knees.

'You bastard,' she whispered threadily.

'I know,' he acknowledged quietly.

The doctor arrived just then, slicing through the
tension in the room by briskly ordering everyone out—
except for Leon, who straightened to shake his hand then
moved stiffly to stand behind the long sofa Jemma was
sitting on. He was a short, stocky man, Greek to the
marrow in his bones, but his grasp of English was superb,
and it was only as he flashed a series of comprehensive
questions at her that Jemma realised hardly anyone
present tonight had spoken in Greek.

Maybe it would have been kinder for her if they had,
she concluded as she suffered the usual physical examination with Leon's sharp eyes on her looking for the
smallest sign of discomfort. Understanding nothing

would have left her sublimely ignorant to what was going on.

Instead, she had heard all, and now knew all. Leon had married her for one reason only. She conveniently suited his urgent requirements.

And it hurt, hurt so much that she couldn't even look at him without feeling ravaged.

'Right,' the doctor said firmly, removing his stethoscope and shoving it into his little black bag. 'You will be pleased to know that there is nothing drastically wrong with either of you!' He smiled briefly at his own joke.

For the life of her, Jemma couldn't smile with him, so she took diversionary tactics, by straightening her dress and levering herself back into a sitting position. She saw Leon's hand snake out to help her, but ignored it. She didn't want him touching her. She didn't want to look at him ever again.

'But,' the doctor continued, 'we are in the middle of a heatwave—even by Greek standards—and partying in your condition, Mrs Stephanades, is perhaps asking for trouble. I suggest you take it easy for a few days. Enjoy making your husband dance attendance on you.' Another joke and another smile he expected to be returned. Leon might have done, but Jemma just lowered her head. 'Then come to my surgery—perhaps Friday?—and we will check you over more thoroughly then.'

Leon saw him out, leaving her alone in the elegant room of his father's house where the beautiful cream and grey décor looked as vapid as she felt. Then her baby kicked, and Jemma smiled sadly to herself. Perhaps not quite that vapid, she allowed, stroking a tender hand over the shifting mound.

The door opened, and she looked up sharply, a fizz of defensive rebelliousness stiffening her spine—only to sag again when she saw not Leon coming back into the room, but the woman who had brought her the glass of water.

'The party goes on, and Leon is grilling the doctor,' she said ruefully. 'So I thought I would come and keep you company.' As gentle in movement as her manner was, she walked across the soft grey-carpeted floor and sat herself down next to Jemma. 'How do you feel?' she asked.

'As well as can be expected, I suppose,' Jemma mocked, not even trying to paper over what had really caused her faint tonight. It would be a waste of time anyway, since this woman had been a party to the row which had followed it in here.

'This is a strong family,' the other woman remarked, 'with each and every one of them a force to be reckoned with. They fight each other as ruthlessly as they fight any battle in business.'

'English,' Jemma murmured irrelevantly. 'They all speak in English.'

'Oh, did you not know? Dimitri is English! Or at least,' she amended, 'he was born in England to Greek parents. They emigrated there after a—series of misfortunes left them with little else to do but start afresh somewhere new.' She was choosing her words carefully. 'He thinks in English—though his Greek is good. But around him, whatever nationality you are, people tend to speak English. He expects it.'

'You seem to know an awful lot about them,' Jemma observed guardedly. 'Does that make you one of them?'

'Ah!' For some reason, she was thoroughly amused. 'No, I am not,' she assured Jemma, 'but I think perhaps it is time we formally introduced ourselves, since manners this evening seem to have been sadly lacking.' She held out her hand. 'I am Melva Markopoulou, a—very old friend of Leon's.'

There was a look in the woman's smiling eyes that Jemma could not interpret—a hint of mockery spiced with something else too intricate to catch. Jemma took the hand and returned shyly, 'Jemma Dav——'

'Stephanades,' a cool voice from the doorway corrected.

'Ah.' Melva's eyes lifted to their intruder. 'Leon, your wife and I were getting to know each other.'

'So I see,' he said, coming further into the room. He was looking at Jemma, but her eyes were blank and staring, focusing on nothing. 'You are feeling more yourself, *agape mou*?'

The endearment made her shudder. But, 'Yes,' she answered, and forced her eyes to focus on a point somewhere between the rigid set of his jaw and the dark brown skin at his throat. 'May we leave now?'

'Of course,' he concurred. 'The car is being brought round now.'

'Good,' she said, and made to get up. Leon reached out to help her and once again Jemma pulled violently away from his touch. 'No,' she rasped, and he stepped back jerkily.

She sensed the other two exchanging glances and knew she had to get away from here before she split wide apart. Her legs were barely supporting her and a hot sense of agitation was disrupting her insides. 'M-my shawl,' she murmured, glancing distractedly around her. 'I c-can't see my shawl——'

'Jemma——'

'Go and collect your wife's shawl, Leon!' Melva inserted quickly. She was on her feet and gently taking Jemma by the arm. 'I shall walk Jemma to the door and we will meet you there.'

There was a short tense moment when Leon thought to argue, then more glances passed between the other two and he sighed impatiently and walked away.

'Please, Jemma!' Melva appealed urgently as soon as he had gone. 'Try not to condemn him out of hand for what took place tonight! It was more his father's fault than anyone's—and of course that avaricious bitch, Anthia's. She has been planning towards the evening—

with a different result, of course—for twenty-eight years!
She is shrewd and clever and totally without scruple.
Leon had to use his weapons carefully or she would have
twisted things to suit herself!'

As Leon had twisted things to suit himself, Jemma
likened. 'Just what is Leon to you,' she demanded, 'that
you come down so completely on his side?'

'She is the woman my father picked out for me to
marry.' Once again, Leon had come upon them without
their realising it. 'But I obliged Melva by refusing to
accede to his threats—did I not, *agape mou*?'

'Don't tease the poor girl, Leon!' Melva scolded.
'Neither of us had any wish to be married to the other,
and it really was as simple as that!'

Laughing up at him, she moved the few steps away
from Jemma to kiss Leon on both cheeks. What she did
next was so deftly done that Jemma wondered afterwards if she would have noticed if she had not been so
hypersensitive to everything happening around her, but
somehow, by the time Melva moved away from Leon
again, Jemma's shawl was in her hands and she turned—
still smiling—to settle carefully the fine white silk around
Jemma's shoulders.

The thoughtful gesture brought a brief wash of tears
to her eyes. She knew she didn't want him to touch her,
and she was saving both of them from any more
discomfort.

'I am well known on the island,' she informed Jemma
gravely. 'If you ever find yourself in need of a friend,
then just ask and you will be directed to my home.'

'I... Thank you,' Jemma whispered, but she knew
she wouldn't take her up on it. She was Leon's friend,
and therefore could not be Jemma's as well.

They drove back to the yacht in complete silence, the
presence of the chauffeur making conversation impossible—of the kind they would have, anyway. And
Jemma was glad. She had no wish to speak to Leon—

or, worse, listen to him while he tried to justify what he had done.

There could be no justification. He had used her. From the moment he had walked back into her life, he had cold-bloodedly planned, calculated and manipulated—everything, from the ruthless way he'd played on her reliance on Trina, to the way he had spent the last three weeks personally supervising her return to good health with his aim focused entirely on this evening. Even the beauty of yesterday had been a coolly thought-out calculation! she realised as hot tears of hurt sped across her eyes. He must have seen her moment of unhappiness as a sign of discontent and the last thing he needed so close to his ultimate aim was an unhappy wife standing by his side! So he'd set out to woo her—woo her into the soft, contented woman he wanted her to be in front of his family, and she, fool that she was, had fallen for it all like a lemming walking blindly towards its own destruction.

And, all the time, he'd known something else that she did not know. He'd known the sex of the child she carried for him. A boy child. More tears burned and she blinked them angrily away. His ultimate weapon in a power game so despicable that it filled her with a bilious disgust of all of them—Leon *and* his family.

The car turned in through the security gates and came to a stop at the yacht. She was trying to open the door even as the engine died.

'Jemma——' Leon's hand on her arm sent a shudder of revulsion through her and she struck it away, not even looking at him as she got out of the car and walked quickly up the steps of the yacht.

She did not stop until she was in their stateroom with the door locked firmly behind her. Then she walked into the bathroom, switched on the shower, stripped off her clothes and stepped beneath the stinging hot spray.

Arriving back in the bedroom, wrapped into her long white towelling robe, she stopped dead, surprised to find Leon standing by the darkened window.

He must have sensed what she was thinking because he murmured, 'I have a pass key to all the locks on board,' without turning to look at her.

Of course, she thought wryly. He would have, wouldn't he? It belonged to him, after all—which by his philosophy meant he had the right to open any door he chose to and damn the invasion of someone else's privacy! Just as he had been damning his invasion of her privacy since he'd decided to make her one of his precious possessions!

Well, never again. 'I'm tired,' she informed him stonily. 'Would you please leave?'

He turned to face her at that, his eyes dark and carefully guarded. 'We have to talk,' he said quietly.

Talk——? Her mouth tightened, losing all of its natural sensual softness. 'The way I read it, it has all already been said.'

'No,' he denied. 'There is a lot you haven't heard. A lot you need to know if you are to understand why I had to do what I did tonight.'

'Used me?' she mocked him bitterly. 'Used our child—and its sex!—as a means to an end, you mean?'

'You have to understand,' he persisted grimly, studiedly ignoring her pained remark. 'I was playing for high stakes tonight. I needed you on my side! Not bristling with indignation and openly despising me as you surely would have been if I had warned you what I was about to do!'

'And that excuses you, does it?' she demanded, blue eyes hot and bitter.

'No,' he conceded. 'It simply explains why I didn't tell you. Look,' he sighed when she continued to wither him with her eyes, 'the company is mine by right! And there is not a person connected with the Leonadis name

who does not know that it belonged to *my* mother, and
her father and grandfather before that! I was even named
Leonadis in anticipation of the day I take over! Of course
I am not going to let anyone cheat me out of what is
mine by right!'

'So you sacrificed my rights for your own.' She nodded
in bitter understanding. 'How honourable!' she added
scathingly.

He winced, but didn't try to defend himself from that
attack. 'I had to do what I had to do!' he insisted instead. 'You heard my father tonight,' he went on harshly.
'His health is failing him. He has known for several
months now that he is no longer fit to run a company
the size of ours with the success he used to enjoy. But
you also heard him say that accepting that point has not
been easy for him. As he feels himself grow weaker he
has to watch me grow stronger! He resents that, nat-
urally! And, in a last-ditch attempt to prove his power
over me—the *only* person worthy of taking over from
him,' he said with angry conceit, 'he dredged up an old
grievance of his—the one where he made the ultimate
coup by marrying me off to Melva Markopoulou and
so uniting two of the most powerful families on this
island! He wanted to bow out on a high note. But, as
always when he tries to bully me, I refused to comply!
So he had that stupid document drawn up and proceeded to threaten me with it. It was a bluff!' he muttered on an angry shrug. 'Just a bluff! He plays these
games with me all the time!' From nowhere, the memory
of the newspaper article saying how his father had tied
Leon's hands over the New York deal popped into
Jemma's mind. 'But eventually he tires of the game, sees
sense, gives in, if you like.' Another shrug. 'He's not a
fool; he knows the company needs me! That I am its
strength and its future! And, left to his own devices, he
would eventually have withdrawn the threat. Except that
Anthia got to hear of it.' His grim mouth tightened. 'And

suddenly Nico is announcing his intention to marry and the damned document is mysteriously made public! Which means my father cannot withdraw it without looking a complete fool. So he begs me again. ''Marry Melva—marry anyone and get yourself a child before Nico beats you to it''!'

'So I was your father's scapegoat,' Jemma concluded, hurting in so many ways that she didn't know which one was the worst. 'How convenient it was to you both that you happened to find me like this!' she mocked. 'The ideal solution to your problem, in fact!'

He looked at her through hard, impatient eyes. 'If I attempted to deny that, you would not believe me, so I will not!' he snapped. 'But I will insist that you believe me when I say that even without the threat hanging over my head the consequences of my discovering you were pregnant with my child would not have changed. I would still have married you, Jemma. I—care for you. I always have.'

'Oh, yes,' she jeered. 'You cared enough to bring me on board this yacht and spend the last two weeks personally supervising my return to robust health so I wouldn't look so pathetic when you made your move tonight!'

He sighed, seeing no way past her bitterness. 'That is not true, Jemma,' he said grimly. 'And when you have calmed down a little, you will see that.'

'All I see,' she retaliated, 'is that everything you have done since you walked back into my life has been one huge deception. Everything,' she repeated thickly, bright tears of hurt and humiliation filling her eyes when she remembered the beauty of the day before. 'You used me,' she whispered tremulously.

'Yes,' he sighed, not even trying to deny it. 'I'm sorry if that hurts you, but—yes——' He sighed again '—I used you.'

And it did hurt, hurt so deeply that she had to turn her back on him so that he would not see the tears burning in her eyes. It was as she turned that she saw it, glittering luridly among her tears, and in an act of sudden violence she snatched up the necklace from where she had tossed it angrily on her dressing-table top earlier, and threw it contemptuously at his chest.

'There,' she said as Leon caught it instinctively. 'One of your props returned to you. But I am afraid you will have to wait several months more for the other, more important one to arrive to complete your victory!'

'Dammit, Jemma!' he exploded, his rough voice shaking as he took a step towards her. 'You are blowing this up larger than——'

'Don't you dare touch me!' she choked, spinning away so that she didn't have to see the look of pained appeal in his eyes.

He muttered something in angry frustration, sending her spine stiff in rejection as he took another step towards her.

'Just leave me alone,' she whispered, pressing her clenched fist against her quivering mouth again.

There was another tense pause, when he seemed to hesitate. She couldn't look at him. If she had done she would have seen the anxiety pulling at his face, and the underlying burn of anger aimed entirely at himself.

Then he sighed heavily. 'All right,' he said. 'If that is what you want.' Then she heard him quietly let himself out of the cabin.

It was then the tears came, hot and pained and scalding. She let them flow, let her hurt and anger and miserable sense of disillusionment pour out with them.

When eventually the storm of weeping subsided, she crawled into the bed and went to sleep still huddled in her robe.

The next morning she got up, dressed herself, plucked the bankroll of drachmas out of the drawer she had put it in and walked outside and right off the yacht. She did not stop to tell anyone where she was going, nor did she even attempt to look for Leon. She needed time, time to be herself again—to learn to be herself again and not the person Leon had been turning her into. So she walked across the quay and out of the security gates enclosing their private moorings, across the busy quayside road and turned down the first street leading away from the harbour, putting herself right out of sight of the yacht as quickly as she could, unaware that Leon stood against the boat's rail, watching her every step of the way, and unaware of the way he snapped out instructions to one of the crew who quickly scuttled after her.

She eventually found herself in what could only be the town square—a big place, flanked by brightly adorned tourist shops and cafés.

She picked a café at random and ordered herself fresh-orange juice and a bottle of chilled water, then sat back simply to let the world go by, her mind swept ruthlessly blank of anything even vaguely contentious.

It felt good, being just a simple tourist enjoying a simple breakfast in a simple café. And slowly, whatever had driven her to walk away as she had eased, until she began to feel a semblance of peace within herself.

After that, she spent the whole morning just wandering around the town, browsing through its narrow busy streets all tightly packed with interesting shops, and, in an absent, purely superficial kind of way, enjoying herself. The Kefallinían people were friendly, warm, and instinctively caring when they noticed her condition, going out of their way to find her a chair if she happened to walk into their shop, asking after her health, the baby's health. Nice people. Genuine people who made her want to weep because they reminded her so much of the man she had married—or the man she'd thought she had married.

Wretchedly, she swung her mind away from that. She didn't want to think of Leon—didn't think she could cope. It wasn't as if he'd told her lies! she reminded herself painfully. He'd just been so cleverly economical with the truth.

And even accepting all of that, accepting that he had married her for very specific reasons of his own did not hurt her as much as the way he had betrayed her with the sex of their baby.

The tears returned, burning at the back of her eyes and forcing her to swallow them down. To think, she scoffed cruelly at herself, I had actually let myself consider that he may love me!

What a fool!

Play with him and you're playing in the big league, someone had warned her once. Well, she'd played, and got burned—not once but twice.

You utter fool!

Could she go on living with a man like that? Did she want to?

It was then she saw it, and she stopped dead, her brain burning with a combination of horror and excitement at the sudden idea which popped unexpectedly into her head.

It was only a tiny place, its windows cluttered with posters advertising the services it sold. But it was the instantly recognisable logo of one of Britain's biggest airline companies that had caught her attention.

With the sun beating down on her uncovered head, she lifted a hand to shade her eyes. Her fingers were trembling. She wasn't surprised. The idea was so incredible that she could barely believe she was actually considering it!

Yet it was tempting—so very tempting—tempting enough to send her feet uncertainly into the shop...

*   *   *

Hot, tired, and ready for a nice cool shower followed by a long rest, Jemma stepped back on to the yacht, hoping Leon was not around to waylay her. Two crewmen watched her come aboard, but other than that she managed to slip quietly back to her own room, the coolness of the air-conditioning a relief after the fierce heat outside.

Walking over to her dressing-table, she dropped down wearily on the stool. She was clutching an envelope in her hand, and she gazed dully at it.

This was it. Her means of escape. Her heart shook, making her sigh heavily.

The price they'd quoted her was in drachmas, yet, even as she'd dug out her roll of notes and begun carefully counting them out, she hadn't really believed she would have enough. She had been wrong. Leon's idea of a few pounds turned out to be the equivalent of a few hundred pounds. Enough—more than enough to buy her a seat on a plane home to England.

It had been so easy—so damned simple that she had to believe it was fate that had sent her into the shop.

Saturday. The day after tomorrow. The envelope held her ticket to freedom. The day after tomorrow she would be flying home and away from Leon. She did not know what she was going to do when she got there, what she was going to live on or even where she was going to stay, but suddenly she knew it was the right thing to do. The only thing to do. She just couldn't stay with a man who could use her so carelessly. It hurt too much.

A sudden knock at the door had her jerking upright, and she spun around, eyes wide, face pale, heart palpitating so badly that she actually felt dizzy with it.

Leon. It had to be Leon. Only he would dare knock in that peremptory way.

'Jemma.' Not a question but a quietly issued command. It was him, and on a sudden spurt of panic she opened her dressing-table drawer and pushed the en-

velope in it, what was left of her money following it
before she turned back to stare at the door.

'Jemma!' His voice was not so quiet this time, and
the knock was sharp with impatience. Pulling herself
together, she schooled her face into a cool mask and
went to open the door.

He looked just the same as always, she noted bitterly.
A little tired maybe, but no sign of guilt spoiling his
handsome face, no hint of remorse. She stared coldly at
him, hating the wretched ache she felt stir inside her,
and turned back into the room. He followed, closing the
door behind him.

'Where have you been?' he asked quietly enough.

Still she bristled. 'Out,' she said, moving jerkily to
close the dressing table drawer when she saw she had
left it open. 'Why?' she challenged, fingers curling
around the smooth cedarwood as she turned back to face
him. 'Do you have a problem with that?'

His eyes had narrowed on her hands, making her heart
thump agitatedly in her breast. Did he know what she'd
done? Could he have found out?

'No,' he answered. 'But it would have been—kinder
if you had warned someone about what you intended to
do.'

'Like you do, you mean?' Her chin came up, her
meaning excruciatingly clear.

Still, he ignored it. 'The doctor said you should rest.
Yet you've been gone for hours. Didn't it occur to you
I may be worried?'

'For whom?' she goaded. 'Me or the child?'

'Both,' he said. Then, with a hint of impatience at
last, 'Listen, I did not come here to argue with you,
Jemma. I am not a fool; I am quite aware that you consider me beneath your contempt at the moment. But,
despite what you prefer to think or believe, I am concerned for your health. I have to attend a meeting this
afternoon,' he went on grimly. 'But I would rather go

to it without worrying whether your desire to punish me could make you foolish enough to go out again and thoroughly exhaust yourself.'

'Then go to your meeting.' She shrugged indifferently. 'Despite what *you* seem to think, I care for this baby's health too. I shall not be leaving the yacht again today.'

'Good,' he murmured. 'And thank you. Your reassurance eases my mind.'

'You trust me to keep my word?' Surprise at his instant acquiescence coloured her tone.

Leon looked steadily at her. 'I have always trusted you, *agape mou*,' he said softly. 'I am the deceiver here, not you, remember?'

On a bleak self-mocking smile he let himself out of her room, leaving her to deal with the sudden rush of guilt she was troubled with. He trusted her. And she was already planning to break that trust.

CHAPTER TWELVE

JEMMA didn't see Leon again that day—thankfully, she told herself firmly when she found her solitary meal that evening an interminable affair where a white-coated steward served small, tempting dishes to her in a concerned effort to inspire her lost appetite.

She had eaten little lunch, had found her usual ability to fall into an undisturbed sleep for a few hours in the afternoon had deserted her, and had in the end wandered restlessly around the yacht, not quite knowing what to do with herself.

You miss him, that little voice inside her head informed her bluntly. And if you can miss him now, when you're riddled with hurt and anger at his deception, then how will you feel when all this hurt fades and you're back in England, having completely cut yourself free of him?

The hurt will never fade, she told that voice when, by ten o'clock, Leon had still not appeared and she took herself off to bed, exhausted by the see-sawing stress of her ravaged emotions. How can it when I only have to feel our son move inside me to remember how cruelly he used us?

Our son. Every time she let herself think the words, her eyes filled with the aching tears of that cruel betrayal. No daughter with blue eyes and her mother's soft mouth. No sweet little girl with golden hair or even her father's dark exotic looks.

But a son, with Leon's bottomless black eyes and charm enough to captivate anyone who came into contact with him. A boy with a sturdy build and an independent mind. Would he have any of her softer genes in him? Or would he be all Greek—all Stephanades—big and strong and heart-rendingly ruthless?

She shuddered, feeling sick but not really understanding why. It wasn't as if she minded whether her baby was a boy or a girl so long as it was whole and healthy. But——

Rape, she realised. It felt like rape. As if someone had come along and coolly robbed her of the most precious part of motherhood.

And it was that which hurt her above everything else, and why she was determined to leave him. He had taken something else from her he could never give back, only this time she minded, minded so much that she could not forgive.

Sleep came suddenly, like the throwing of a switch, as if her brain had taken the decision to shut her off from the stresses of the last two days.

She slept long and deeply, waking in the morning feeling decidedly sluggish and with a banging head. Remembering she was to see the doctor this morning, she dragged herself out of bed and into the bathroom, grimacing when she caught sight of her pale, listless face. The last twenty-four hours had effectively wiped out two weeks' convalescence.

Which only helped to confirm one thing—it was the man who was her weakness, not her health.

She took her time in the shower, letting the tepid water gush over her hair and down her body for ages in the hope that the refreshing spray would disperse her headache.

It was only as she walked back into her bedroom fifteen minutes later wrapped in a towel and with her hair slicked to her skull that something about the movement of the yacht caught at her attention, and she frowned, moving to the window to glance out.

Nothing. Her body jarred on shock. She should be looking across the clear waters of the bay of Argostólion towards the misted green hills above Lixoúrion. But there was nothing in front of her but a bright, glinting stretch of water for as far as she could see.

'No,' she murmured, beginning to tremble all over. 'No!' They couldn't have moved during the night—she would have heard the engines! Been awoken by the movement! She had an appointment with the doctor! Leon could not have moved them!

Turning, she ran to her wardrobe and grabbed at the first thing that came to hand—a baggy white cotton T-shirt that finished halfway down her thighs—only belatedly remembering to add a pair of cotton briefs before she was rushing through the door.

She ran up on to the deck then stopped, her eyes gone slightly wild as she searched the far horizon for a glimpse of land. There was none. She turned, heart pumping, and ran back inside, only to skid to a halt at the open door to the main salon.

Leon was there, sitting on one of the elegant sofas, bent forward so that he could rest his elbows on his spread knees. He was wearing his grey shorts and nothing else, she noted pensively—as if the casualness of his attire was making a statement in itself.

'W-where are we?' she gasped out breathlessly.

He looked up, his eyes full of dark shadows in his grim face. 'Nowhere,' he said, looking away from her and back at his hands. 'Anywhere.' He shrugged as if he couldn't care less.

It was then she saw them spread out on the low table beside him, and her heart leapt to her throat, eyes spiralling out of focus then back in again on the items lying there. Her passport. Her wallet containing her bit of English money. Her thin roll of drachmas and, most damning of all, the envelope containing her ticket away from him.

'You went through my drawer!' she accused him hoarsely.

'I could not let you do it, Jemma. No matter how much you hate me, you need me right now. I could not let you do it,' he repeated grimly.

Her legs lost their ability to support her, and she had to feel her way to the nearest chair and drop heavily into it.

'How—how did you find out?'

'I had a man follow you yesterday, but he could not go in the travel agents and enquire which flight you had booked without drawing attention to us.' He grimaced. 'The Stephanades name is too well known on this island,' he explained. 'It could have caused quite a sensation if it had come out that my wife was trying to run away from me.'

'So you waited until I was asleep,' she whispered, 'then quietly rifled through my private things to get your information.' Her contempt showed at this latest invasion of her privacy.

Leon just shrugged. 'And what did I find?' he mocked, lancing her with a sardonic look. 'I found that my unending patience in waiting until you were asleep before trying to discover just what you were up to was a complete waste of time, because you didn't book your flight under the Stephanades name, did you? You didn't need to while your passport still bears your maiden name. You really should learn to come to terms with who you are now, *agape mou*,' he added cynically, 'for in this case just the simple mention of who you really are would have got you on the first flight off the island, instead of having to wait two whole days to do it.'

'Except that it is a name I have no wish to be associated with!' she threw bitterly at him.

'Too late,' he drawled. 'It is already yours and will remain so for the rest of your life.'

'Not if I decide otherwise.' She jumped up, disturbed by the deadly serious look in his eyes. 'There's such a thing as divorce, you know.'

'Not with me, there isn't,' he stated.

'Not until I have safely delivered your son, you mean!' Moving jerkily, she went over to the fridge to get herself a bottle of chilled water. 'After all, he is the only reason I'm here at all!'

'Not true,' he denied.

She spun on him. 'Of course it's true,' she declared, her fingers working agitatedly at the stubborn bottle-top. 'It was always true from the moment you asked the doctor back in London what the sex of our baby was! Dammit!' she sobbed out wretchedly. 'I can't do this!'

Tears of angry frustration blurring her eyes, she held the bottle out to him. Leon came to his feet and took it from her, easily twisting the cap open and pouring the water into a glass before handing it to her.

He stood, watching her gulp thirstily at the drink, then said quietly, 'I did not ask the doctor anything about the child. I only asked him about your health.'

Her angry blue eyes scoffed at him. 'Then how else would you learn the sex of our child?'

'I don't know it,' he said. 'I lied.'

Jemma went still, staring at him in stunned disbelief. Then, 'What?' she gasped.

'I lied,' he repeated flatly, taking the empty glass from her and putting it aside. 'I needed to leave Anthia and Nico with no leg to stand on, so——' he shrugged '—I lied about knowing the child's sex. It was only when I saw the effect the lie had on you that I realised how unforgivably cruel I had been by using it.'

Jemma began to shake. 'I don't believe you,' she breathed.

'I didn't think you would.' His smile was brief and rueful. 'Which is why I have not tried to tell you before now. After all, why should you believe me after the way I set you up for all of that?'

She stared into his face, looking—searching for the truth in those impossibly black eyes, then shook her head. 'You're lying now—not then,' she said, wrapping her arms about her body as if she needed their protection. 'You wouldn't dare make such a claim without being sure it was the truth because there is a fifty-fifty chance that I will give birth to a girl, and then it would be you left without a leg to stand on, looking the fool. No company, nothing.'

He had to gall to laugh, then shake his head ruefully. 'You are quite wrong, you know,' he attested. 'Personally, I couldn't give a damn what sex our child is so long as it is healthy. You see, the Leonadis Corporation is already mine. My father officially signed it over to me yesterday—with relief, I might add, because I managed to get him out of such a sticky situation without making him look like the fool. Seeing Nico taking his place was enough to give him nightmares. But Nico is his son, too. He had no wish to hurt his feelings by being forced to tell him he was not fit for the job.'

'So my feelings were sacrificed instead!'

'Now that I have no excuse for,' he quietly acknowledged.

'You hurt me!'

'Yes.' He acknowledged that also.

'You deliberately set out to use me!'

'Yes,' quietly again. 'Forgive me. Please?'

'How can I?' she cried. 'If this baby is a boy, I will never be sure when you told the truth!' Her blue eyes filled with wretched tears. 'I can never trust you again, Leon!'

Sighing, he reached for her, but she shrugged him away. 'No,' she protested. 'Don't touch me.'

When he touched her, she weakened. Hadn't she always been weak with him?

'Then at least listen to me,' he asked. 'Please, Jemma,' he begged when she went to turn away. 'Listen—just listen? And when I have finished, if you still want to leave me I'll—arrange it.' Even Jemma in her wretchedness heard that hesitation in his voice for what it was.

She lifted her eyes to look at him. 'Another lie, Leon?' she challenged.

'No,' he denied. Then on a grimace, 'Perhaps,' he conceded. 'Letting you go is not what I want to do and, selfish swine that I am, I am not sure that I can do it just like that.' Grimly, he raked frustrated fingers through his hair. His face was pale, and she could see the strain of sleepless nights pulling at his features.

Her heart began to ache—for herself or for him she wasn't sure, but it made her want to weep. Shakily, she put up a hand to cover her eyes. 'I feel so wretched!' she choked.

'Come and sit down.' His voice sounded gruff, and the hand he curled around her arm was trembling a little. She let him lead her over to one of the soft cushioned sofas and guide her into it. Then he pulled up a matching chair and sat down in front of her, bending to place his forearms on his knees while he waited for her to get a hold of herself.

Then, 'Jemma,' he said quietly, 'I love you.'

She stiffened in instant rejection. 'You don't know the meaning of the word!' she denounced, bitterly denouncing, too, that weak flutter of joy her heart responded with.

'I thought I didn't,' he agreed. 'I thought I never wanted to know, until I met you.' His smile was heavy with irony, then was gone as he looked into her tear-washed eyes. 'But I missed you when I was in New York,' he murmured softly. 'Nothing seemed worth breaking my neck for when I did not have you to rush back to.'

'You seemed to do well enough,' she remarked, remembering the article in the newspaper that had so sung his praises.

'That is because I hardly ever went home,' he explained. 'I just bit people's heads off and made the kind of reckless decisions that should have been the finish of me.'

'Then it was lucky for you that it went the other way,' she mocked that explanation acidly.

'Yes.' He deliberately ignored her scorn. 'Then all this stuff with Nico blew up, and my father was on the phone panicking because Nico has announced his intention to marry and that stupid document he had drawn up to make me toe his line was suddenly backfiring on him because Anthia knew about it, and, although he loves her—almost to distraction—he also knows of her insane need to possess, if not for herself then for her son, anything that was once my mother's. It is not entirely greed that drives her,' he admitted. 'She was my father's first love—his only love! But he sold her out for a big purse, and if she ever forgave him for it she never forgave my mother—or me for that matter.'

Another grimace, and Jemma found herself wondering painfully what kind of childhood he must have had, with a stepmother who resented the very sight of him.

'Being well aware of this,' he went on, 'through the years, my father had been very careful never to give her the slightest hope that Nico will ever inherit anything that belongs to the Leonadis family. There are other things,' he explained. 'Other ventures which are kept entirely separate from the main corporation. Ventures my father set up and built on his own merit. Those are Nico's for the taking. He knows it—I know it! Nico was, until recently, content with what he knew was to be his. But Anthia wasn't. This chance appeared and she took it with both hands by quickly marrying Nico off and making that document known to anyone who mattered.'

For a moment, angry frustration roughened his voice. 'My father was now facing the prospect of having to make the biggest climb-down of his life by withdrawing that document. I couldn't let him do it!' he muttered. 'He is old and he is ill, and, though we may not always see eye to eye, I love him and I am proud of all he has achieved with his life. I could not let him go out on such a low light.' He took in a deep breath then let it out again. '"Marry Melva", he begged. "Marry anyone but get me out of this mess"! And I realised that there was only one woman I could think of marrying—only one woman I wanted to marry! You!' he stated huskily. 'You and only you.'

He was looking at her, willing her to lift her eyes to his, but she didn't, keeping them lowered on her twisting hands.

He sighed heavily, then went on. 'So I came back to London to see you. I meant to explain all of this to you then ask for your help—keep it all as honest as I could. But—you know how I found you, Jemma!' he declared. 'Pregnant with my child! Weakened by sickness and so obviously struggling to survive that suddenly my priorities changed! Or maybe they were only excuses in the first place, I don't know.' He shrugged. 'But from the moment I set eyes on you again it was you I was concerned about. Your health, your happiness and wellbeing! Blow my father, I thought to myself. He can stew for a while; Jemma needs me—and it felt so good to be needed by you,' he chanted huskily, 'that I proceeded to put the rest of it to the back of my mind because I was enjoying myself too much making up for all those miserable months in New York when I missed you so badly. I'll explain the rest of it to her tomorrow, I kept telling myself. And the tomorrow became another tomorrow and another and another because we were happy and I didn't want to spoil it with what had really become such an insignificant part of why I married you at all! Then suddenly I had run out of tomorrows!' he bit out angrily. 'And it hit me hard the morning my father came to the yacht that I had left it too late; that whatever I said now was going to hurt you because it looked so damned calculated!'

He ran a hand over his eyes, eyes that had been alight with a burning sincerity all the way through his long explanation.

'Jemma,' he pleaded, 'you have to believe me when I say that I never wanted to hurt you. It just—reached a point where there was no other way out without hurting you! But, if you will let me, I will try my best to make it up to you.'

He didn't know it, but he had already gone a long way to doing just that. Yet——

Confused by the wrangle of emotions churning inside her, she got up and walked over to gaze out of the window.

'I lied, Jemma, about knowing the sex of our child,' he said quietly. 'My father knows I lied. I told him before I would let him sign anything over to me.'

Surprised, she glanced at him. 'And he didn't mind you lying to him in public like that?'

He shook his head. 'He only wanted to save his own face. If we have a daughter it will be my credibility placed in question, not his.'

'Which could happen if we do have a daughter,' she pointed out.

Oddly, Leon smiled. 'Actually,' he murmured rather ruefully, 'you quoted fifty-fifty odds at me on that event happening. But,' he confessed, 'I feel it only fair to warn you that there has not been a female born into the Stephanades line for five generations, which must widen the odds considerably.'

'In your favour.'

He nodded. 'Which does not help me in convincing you that I lied—does it?'

'No, it doesn't,' Jemma agreed, turning to stare at the rich blue Ionian Sea sparkling in the morning sun. Yet she was beginning to believe him. Why she was not quite sure except, perhaps, because she wanted to believe him, needed to if she was going to be able to forgive him and put all of this aside, try to pick up the pieces of their relationship from here, but...

But what? she asked herself bleakly. What exactly is it you're so upset about? A lie that, since you've been told it is a lie, has lost its power to wound? Or the fact that you trusted him so utterly that when he let you down you couldn't take it?

What has changed? What has really changed over the last twenty-four hours other than you've witnessed a more ruthless side to his character and have been made painfully aware that he is capable of going to any lengths to win?

And what else would you expect of a man like him? He's strong. So strong that even his father leans on him. *You* lean on him! You barely exist when he isn't near you—last night proved that, when you sat here on this yacht, pining for him even while you were hating him.

As she turned back to look at him, her heart gave a painful squeeze when she saw he was sitting there with his wide shoulders hunched, dark head lowered in grim contemplation of his hands again. He looked oddly vulnerable sitting there like that—cut off and alone, as perhaps, she realised, strong men had to be if they were to maintain that air of strength.

Yet she didn't like it. It hurt something precious inside her to see him like that. It wasn't the man she had come to know so well, that other warm, caring and crushingly gentle man he had always been when alone with her.

The man who claimed he loved her.

Dared she believe him? Dared she take the ultimate risk and let herself trust in that love?

She swallowed thickly, her heart beginning to drum with need and fear and a host of other emotions she could not begin to separate as, warily, she let her defences come tumbling down.

'Leon?' she asked, her tense throat working as she watched his head come up, expression carefully guarded as it focused on her. Lips dry and unsteady, she ran her tongue over them then whispered thickly, 'If I tell you I love you, will you break my heart?'

His eyes closed—on what she didn't know, but she felt the power of it wash right over her. Then he was on his feet and coming towards her. 'They say beauty is only skin-deep,' he responded huskily as he reached for her. 'But with you it glows from every living cell. Thank you. And no,' he answered her question, 'I will never break your beautiful heart. How can I, when it is so precious to me?'

'Then just hold me,' she begged. 'I need to feel you holding me.'

His body became the rock she clung to as he drew her into his arms. She wound her arms around his body, fingers splaying across the muscled blades of his shoulders, and, sighing shakily, she lifted her mouth for his kiss. He took it passionately, stirring her into bright, vibrant life as no other man had ever managed to do.

And there it was, she acknowledged from somewhere within the deep abiding warmth of his embrace. The reason why she was here at all. This man, his touch. Her catalyst. She could deny him nothing.

'It frightens me, what you do to me,' she told him breathlessly when at last he eased the hungry pressure. 'You tear my senses to shreds. I can't resist you!'

'You think it is any different for me? *Feel* me!' he commanded. 'I am trembling.' And as he pressed himself against her she could feel the tremors shaking him—even his hands as he ran them beneath her shirt, up over her hips then caressingly across the child before cupping her breasts. 'I love you, Jemma,' he declared. 'Please, whatever else you doubt about me, do not doubt my love.'

She looked up at him, blue eyes searching impassioned black ones for a hint—the slightest sign—that he was being anything but sincere. But it was all there. The man she had come to admire and respect for the strong, powerful personality he was. The man she had come to love deeply and depend upon so totally that she knew she couldn't live without him now, even if she wanted to, which she didn't. And the man she knew—had always known, no matter what else got in their way—cared for her. A care he was now insisting had turned to love. A love she did not have the strength to turn her back on, especially now when she could see it glowing warmly in his eyes.

'I do believe you,' she said at last. And she did. At last she dared to let herself believe.

'And forgive?' he asked. 'Can you do that too?'

'Oh, yes.' She smiled a wryly rueful smile. 'I can forgive you anything when you hold me like this!' she confessed.

'Then I have a better idea,' he said. 'Bed,' he decided, black eyes gleaming as he bent to swing her into his arms. 'There I can hold you much closer and for much longer and therefore receive a deeper forgiveness!'

'But—what about my appointment with the doctor?' she protested as he began striding towards the door.

'Blow the doctor!' he grunted. 'I need you right now more than you need him!'

'But——!'

He kissed her, his mouth covering her own to muffle out any other protest she might have been considering. And the next time she came up for air he was lowering her on to her own bed, still rumpled from last night's sleep.

He left her to go and close and lock the cabin door. When he back back she was smiling ruefully. 'Who has the pass key?' she asked.

'I do, of course,' he grinned, and came to lie beside her.

Strangely, the fever of passion had passed, leaving them without its raging flame to hide behind. A silence settled around them. Leon seemed suddenly extraordinarily concerned in smoothing her long hair out behind her. And she found a similar interest in the absent combing of the silk dark hair at his chest.

'Where would you like to live?' he asked suddenly. 'London? Athens? New York?'

She glanced at him from beneath her lashes. 'You choose,' she offered. 'I have no personal preference so long as we are together.'

'Mmm, my sentiments exactly,' he agreed, brushing a kiss across her cheek. 'But we have to make our base somewhere, if only until the baby is born. After that, you both travel with me wherever I go,' he decreed, adding grimly, 'I do not ever want to go through another separation like the age I spent in New York without you.'

Jemma bit down lightly on her bottom lip, then said softly, 'I missed you too. A million times I wanted to call you up and tell you how frightened and alone I felt. But——' She sighed, unable to explain.

'But you could not because you did not think I cared enough,' he finished for her.

She shook her head. 'No,' she denied. 'I knew you cared, Leon. I never, ever doubted that you cared for me. But caring was not enough—not with a baby coming and you being so very against marriage. It wouldn't have been fair on you, would it?'

'And was it fair on you,' he posed, 'that you should have to cope alone?'

She shrugged. 'That business with Cassie and Josh obsessed me. I just couldn't see you reacting any differently than he had.'

'Did you do it deliberately?' he asked.

'No!' she denied, her eyes jerking up to clash angrily with his. 'How could you think I would do such a thing?'

'I did not,' he denied. 'I just asked the question, that's all. And you answered it.' He gave a 'that's the end of that' shrug.

'You believe me—just like that?' she choked.

His eyes, sombre beneath their lazy lids, held on to hers. 'Did you not know?' he mocked her gently. 'I would believe you if you told me the world was square. You are the most honest person I know, *agape mou*.'

'Oh,' she said, and for some stupid reason felt tears press at her eyes again.

'Don't.' Sighing, he pulled her to him, curving his body protectively around her. 'Don't cry,' he commanded. 'God, you have no idea what it does to me to see you unhappy! Of course I know you did not deliberately set me up!' he scolded. 'I can do simple arithmetic too, you know! And, even if you had done it deliberately,' he then added wryly, 'I would not have cared less. My life is incomplete without you, my darling,' he murmured softly, coming to lean over her so that she could see the sincerity burning in his eyes. 'I learned that in New York.' He kissed her gently. 'Here I am complete.' He kissed her again. 'With you—anywhere with you.' Another kiss, soft and lingering. 'You,' he murmured. 'You— you—you.'

HARLEQUIN PRESENTS®

HARLEQUIN ◈ PRESENTS®

Dark secrets...

forbidden desires...

scandalous discoveries...

an enthralling six-part saga from a bright new talent!

HEARTS OF FIRE
by Miranda Lee

This exciting new family saga is set in the glamorous world
of opal dealing in Australia. *HEARTS OF FIRE* unfolds over
six books, revealing the passion, scandal, sin and hope that
exist between two fabulously rich families. Each novel
features its own gripping romance—and you'll also be
hooked by the continuing story of Gemma Smith's search
for the truth about her real mother, and the priceless
Black Opal....

Coming next month

Book 2: *Desire & Deception*

Jade's father had hired Kyle Armstrong as the new
marketing manager of Whitmore Opals—the job Jade
coveted.... She tried to hate him, but her resentment kept
turning into desire, until Jade didn't know *how* she felt
about Kyle! Would she end up fighting, or kissing him—and
wasn't that how Gemma felt toward Jade's adoptive brother,
Nathan? Two independent women, two forceful sexy men...
Would their relationships be ruled by anger or passion?

Harlequin Presents: you'll want to know what happens next!

Available in August wherever Harlequin books are sold.

FLYAWAY VACATION SWEEPSTAKES!

This month's destination:

Glamorous LAS VEGAS!

Are you the lucky person who will win a free trip to Las Vegas? Think how much fun it would be to visit world-famous casinos... to see star-studded shows...to enjoy round-the-clock action in the city that never sleeps!

The facing page contains two Official Entry Coupons, as does each of the other books you received this shipment. Complete and return all the entry coupons—**the more times you enter, the better your chances of winning!**

Then keep your fingers crossed, because you'll find out by August 15, 1995 if you're the winner! If you are, here's what you'll get:

- Round-trip airfare for two to exciting Las Vegas!
- 4 days/3 nights at a fabulous first-class hotel!
- $500.00 pocket money for meals and entertainment!

Remember: The more times you enter, the better your chances of winning!*

*NO PURCHASE OR OBLIGATION TO CONTINUE BEING A SUBSCRIBER NECESSARY TO ENTER. SEE REVERSE SIDE OF ANY ENTRY COUPON FOR ALTERNATIVE MEANS OF ENTRY.

VLV KAL

FLYAWAY VACATION
SWEEPSTAKES

OFFICIAL ENTRY COUPON

This entry must be received by: JULY 30, 1995
This month's winner will be notified by: AUGUST 15, 1995
Trip must be taken between: SEPTEMBER 30, 1995-SEPTEMBER 30, 1996

YES, I want to win a vacation for two in Las Vegas. I understand the prize includes round-trip airfare, first-class hotel and $500.00 spending money. Please let me know if I'm the winner!

Name_____

Address _____ Apt. _____

City   State/Prov.   Zip/Postal Code

Account #_____

Return entry with invoice in reply envelope.

© 1995 HARLEQUIN ENTERPRISES LTD.   CLV KAL